SPY GODDESS

To Hawaii, with Love

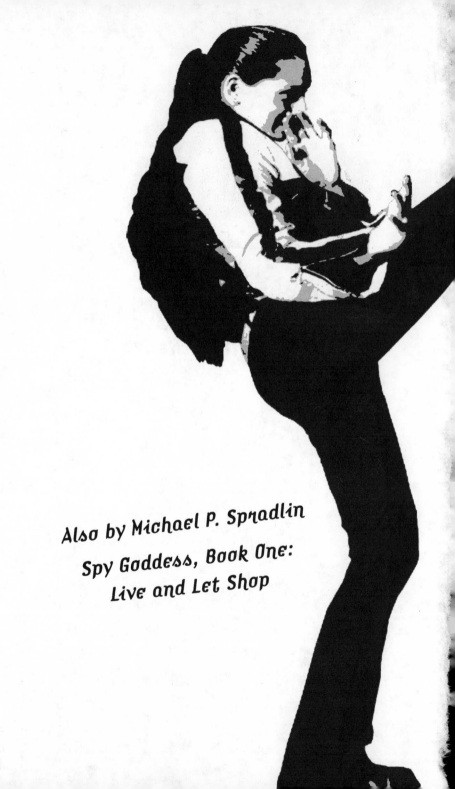

Also by Michael P. Spradlin

Spy Goddess, Book One:
Live and Let Shop

SPY GODDESS

BOOK TWO

To Hawaii, with Love

MICHAEL P. SPRADLIN

HarperCollins*Publishers*

www.harperteen.com

Library of Congress Cataloging-in-Publication Data
Spradlin, Michael P.

  To Hawaii, with love / by Michael P. Spradlin.— 1st ed.

    p. cm. — (Spy goddess ; bk. 2)

  Summary: Headstrong Rachel Buchanan and her friends sneak away from Blackthorn Academy and set out to find a mysterious artifact before it falls into the hands of her nemesis, Simon Blankenship, a journey that takes them to the volcanic shores of Hawaii.

  ISBN-10: 0-06-059410-1 (trade bdg.)

  ISBN-13: 978-0-06-059410-7 (trade bdg.)

  ISBN-10: 0-06-059411-X (lib. bdg.)

  ISBN-13: 978-0-06-059411-4 (lib. bdg.)

  [1. Boarding schools—Fiction. 2. Schools—Fiction. 3. Spies—Fiction. 4. Friendship—Fiction. 5. Supernatural— Fiction. 6. Hawaii—Fiction.] I. Title. II. Series.

PZ7.S7645Toah 2006   2005005076

[Fic]—dc22   CIP

                                      AC

Typography by R. Hult

1 2 3 4 5 6 7 8 9 10

First Edition

To

Kelly Ann Spradlin,

for always doing the heavy lifting.
—MS

TABLE OF CONTENTS

PROLOGUE

Kuzbekistan, A.D. *360*

Flavius, Emperor of the Roman Empire, knelt at the altar of the underground temple, his head bowed in prayer. Prayers that had, so far, gone unanswered. The battle was nearly over. From far away he could hear the clang of steel and the shouts of fighting, dying legionnaires. Soon his lines would be overrun. The forces of Queen Naromi had nearly decimated his army. He was a beaten man.

Flavius stood. On his head was a shiny silver helmet with two long pointed horns that extended from each side. He wore a flowing black robe and around his neck hung a solid gold medallion. Carved into the medallion was a silhouette of a bull's head. He looked every inch the High Priest of Mithras that he was. He wondered why his god had deserted him.

He heard a noise in the temple behind him and turned to see Gaius, his aide-de-camp, striding toward him across the temple floor. Gaius reached the altar, knelt, and saluted, his thumb touching the center of his chest, fingers spread, his arm then moving outward. The Mithrian salute.

"Praise be to Mithras, my lord," said Gaius.

"Praise be to Mithras," said Flavius. He grasped his beloved aide by the shoulders and pulled him to his feet.

"Did you summon the Centurions?" he asked.

"Yes, Emperor. As you commanded. They shall arrive momentarily," Gaius said.

"And what of my ships?" Flavius asked.

"They are provisioned and ready to leave when the order is given," he said.

Flavius sighed in relief.

"Well done, Gaius. You have served me ably these many years. When the Centurions depart, you are to leave with them. Return to Rome if possible. Try to salvage whatever life for yourself that you can."

"My lord, my duty is to remain here with you!"

"I release you from that duty, Gaius. You have served Mithras with honor. You must go."

"Emperor, it is not over. Surely Mithras will provide . . ."

Flavius shook his head.

"Mithras has found me unworthy of his power. He will one day rise again, when a new successor is chosen. Our duty to him now is to complete our last sacred mission."

Gaius started to protest but was interrupted by the sound of the Centurions entering the temple. Seven men, their armor blood-spattered and covered in dust and grime, strode to the altar, where they all saluted and knelt before Flavius.

"Praise be to Mithras," they murmured in unison.

Flavius returned the salute and stood before the Centurions. They were the best and bravest of his army. All of them were strong and capable men, fearless in battle, and wholly willing to die for the cause.

"You have been chosen," said Flavius as they knelt before him. "The battle is lost, and our dark lord Mithras will soon return to the underworld to await his next ascension. Your exceptional bravery and devotion are called upon to carry out one last mission in his name."

Flavius took a golden statue off the altar and handed it to the first man in line. The image was a bull seated on its hindquarters, its horns encrusted with diamonds and rubies.

"Quintus, you have been my most faithful and dedicated commander. You have served the Empire and Mithras with honor and distinction. Do you accept this last task I ask of you?"

"As you command it, my lord, so it shall be," said Quintus.

Flavius gave Quintus a small parchment scroll from the pocket of his robe.

"Do not accept this mission lightly. Quintus, you especially will travel the greatest distance, to a faraway land. You will encounter many dangers, but you must succeed. Will you still undertake this mission in the name of Mithras?" said Flavius.

3

"I swear it shall be done," said Quintus, bowing his head before the Emperor.

Flavius smiled. He turned back to the altar and picked up a silver chalice bedecked with rubies and sapphires. He handed it to the Centurion next to Quintus and then gave him an identical small parchment scroll.

"Each of you will be given one of the Seven Treasures of Mithras. Once you are aboard your ships you may open your scrolls, but not before. It will provide you with details and guidance as to where each treasure is to be hidden. It will not be easy. Mithras has commanded that many of you will travel great distances, some of you to lands yet undiscovered, but with his aid you shall arrive at your destination. There you will build a temple in his name and keep the treasure hidden from the forces of Etherea. One day, Mithras will choose a new vessel for this fight. That man shall gather the treasures together again and use their power to summon our lord forth to rule over the Earth!"

Flavius finished his speech and, one by one, the Centurions took the objects that Flavius handed them—the golden medallion from around his neck, a parchment scroll wrapped around a solid silver rod, a spear, a chalice—until each man held one of the sacred objects in his hands.

In the background the sounds of battle drew closer. Screaming horses, thundering chariots, and the clash of steel on steel could be heard clearly, even in the underground temple.

"Each of you understands what you must do?" said Flavius.

Each of the Centurions nodded.

"Then go, and may Mithras guide you safely on your journey."

The Centurions stood and saluted. Quickly they filed to the back of the temple and up the stairs to the surface. In a moment they were gone, leaving Flavius and Gaius alone in the temple.

Flavius turned to the altar again; a great book lay upon it. He took up his stylus and wrote several lines on the last page, then gently closed it. Reaching into the pocket of his robe, he removed a large ruby the size of a small chicken egg and held it above his head. Light from the torches that lit the temple caused the ruby to glitter and dance in his hand.

"I seal the *Book of Seraphim* with the Bloodstone of Mithras," he said. He took the ruby and placed it in a clasp on the very center of the front cover of the *Book of Seraphim*. It was the largest jewel on the cover, and was surrounded by seven bright smaller rubies at various points on the face of the book. The effect was dazzling.

Flavius's shoulders seemed to sag. He turned and looked at Gaius.

"It is time for you to leave," said Flavius.

"But, my lord, surely we can escape. We can take the book and . . ."

Flavius shook his head.

"No, Gaius. It is done. Mithras has commanded me. I was foolish to think myself worthy of his power, and to die here shall be my fate. Fear not, my friend. One day long after our bones have turned to dust, he will choose a new champion, and when the time is right, that champion will bring him forth and the blood of Etherea will darken the sky and the power of Mithras will raise an army of followers that will lay waste to all who oppose him! But we shall not live to see it, so you must go. Keep the word of Mithras alive and one day our descendants will know his glory! But you must hurry!"

Outside the temple the sounds of battle grew louder. The cries of dying Roman soldiers seemed to echo off the temple walls. Gaius looked at his Emperor one last time and then sadly turned and strode across the floor to the steps. As he climbed out of the darkness, he could swear that he heard the cry of a furious bull fill the temple, echoing off the walls until it seemed the sound was all around him. Frightened, Gaius risked only a quick glance back. For a moment he thought he saw a swirling mist rise up out of the temple floor near the altar. He was sure his mind was playing tricks, for he seemed to see something not quite a man, not quite a beast, but a hideous half-man, half-beast materialize in the mist.

Gaius looked away and quickened his pace up the temple steps. Just as he reached the surface, he heard evil-sounding laughter fill the temple.

Then he heard Flavius scream. It was an unholy scream full of rage and pain, as if the soul was being torn away from its body. It haunted Gaius for the rest of his days.

CHAPTER ONE

Future Goddesses of America

There is a crazy man after me. Not just your normal crazy man, either. Not some simple ordinary type of crazy, like a celebrity stalker or someone who gets messages from outer space. This is a guy who thinks that he can *rule* the *world*. We're talking Adolf Hitler–type looniness here.

Many years ago this guy accidentally discovered an ancient temple in a Middle Eastern desert that was once dedicated to a Roman god named Mithras. When he discovered the temple, either he unleashed some kind of supernatural force that made him nutso or his obsession with what he found caused him to check himself into the Crazy Hotel.

Oh, and did I also mention that he thinks I'm the living reincarnation of the Goddess Etherea? I told you: wacko.

Anyway, whatever he thinks or however he came to think it, the main thing is he wants me dead. Somehow he's got the idea that I'm the only thing standing between him and world domination.

His name is Simon Blankenship. For many years he was a member of an elite, clandestine group of U.S. secret agents called the Blackthorn Squad, along with my headmaster and teacher, Jonathon Kim. Mr. Kim was with Blankenship when he discovered the temple, but whatever happened in there didn't make *him* crazy. I know this because Mr. Kim is probably the most centered and noncrazy person I know.

Mr. Kim is the headmaster at Blackthorn Academy, the boarding school in Pennsylvania that I attend. Well, "attend" is not exactly the right word. Saying you "attend" a school would imply that you had a choice in whether or not to go there, whereas I really didn't. See, I was in a little trouble with the law and this judge said I could either go to the school or go to Juvenile Detention. Since I figured that a young girl from a wealthy Beverly Hills family wouldn't do so well in Juvie, I chose the school. Yep. I fought the law and the law won. I've been here for just about two months now and it's been "interesting," to say the least.

I've had to work every other day in the school's kitchen, attend a full load of very difficult, really weird classes, and start to learn Tae Kwon Do. And for the most part I've been denied my beloved Internet access. Also, I discovered that the school secretly sits on top of one of the most sophisticated crime labs and secret-agent hangouts in the world. That's because Mr. Kim, the former secret agent, established the school to train students to become members of a worldwide network devoted to stopping Blankenship and his Mithrians. Some of the upperclassmen here at Blackthorn, the ones who belong to the "Top Floor" section, go on missions with agents to help with surveillance or sting operations. That's way cool. Mr. Kim won't let me into Top Floor yet, but I'm wearing him down.

Along with some of the other students here I also helped Mr. Kim recover a very rare, ancient book that Blankenship had tried to steal. Of course, it turned out that Mr. Kim had actually switched the books ahead of time, so Blankenship ended up with a fake. Only, Blankenship doesn't know it's fake. He thinks it's real. Which is a good thing for us.

That was when Blankenship, who now calls himself Mithras, swore that he would seek his revenge on me. Like I said, he thinks that I am the reincarnation of the goddess Etherea, who, according to legend, was sent by the gods to banish Mithras to the underworld.

Did I mention he was crazy?

"No, Rachel, you must cock your hip first, then sweep your arm like this and throw the attacker across your leg, like this," said Mr. Kim. He grabbed the front of my *do bak* and sent me sprawling to the mat. I felt the air whoosh out of my lungs. Again.

From where he was watching, Alex Scott let out a chuckle. Alex is a second-degree black belt in Tae Kwon Do, and while he's pretty strong and brave and stuff, he's really kind of a pain in my backside. He's always laughing at me, because for the most part, I'm a total klutz. I gave him my best stink-eye as I struggled back to my feet.

Brent Christian, who was almost a black belt, stood next to Alex. Brent was different. He was quiet, soft-spoken, and gentle, and he never laughed at me when I exhibited my less-than-graceful nature. Also, it didn't hurt that he has this kind of young Colin Farrell look going, either.

It was 7 A.M. and I was in the school's *do jang*, taking another private Tae Kwon Do lesson from Mr. Kim. *Do jang* is a Korean word that means "the place of the way." It's a training room where students practice. Since all the fuss with Blankenship, Mr. Kim had decided that we needed to accelerate my martial arts training. So I met him at 6:30 every morning in the *do jang*, where he drilled me relentlessly on the patterns and taught me self-defense moves. Alex and Brent came along most mornings to help out.

There were two problems with this as far as I was concerned. The first was that I am not a morning person. It was bad enough that everyone at Blackthorn is an early-riser, go-getter type. I mean, they serve breakfast at eight o'clock for crying out loud. I can't possibly form a coherent thought before 10 A.M. The second problem was that since Mr. Kim had started these "extra training sessions," most of the "extra training" involved me landing on my keister. Because Mr. Kim, in addition to being a superspy and the headmaster, is one of the very best martial artists in the world. He is a Ninth Dan in Tae Kwon Do, an Aikido master, and not only that, he is a personal friend of Jackie Chan. Needless to say, I was a little overmatched. But Mr. Kim felt it was important that I learn as much as I could, as fast as I could.

Don't get me wrong. There aren't any shortcuts to learning a martial art. Believe me, because I looked for them. All you could do was train over and over until the movements and patterns became second nature. So Mr. Kim's solution to my problem was simply to train more. And when Mr. Kim felt something was important, he had a way of making *you* feel it was important. Only, somehow he made it all seem like it was your idea. He was a tricky one, that Mr. Kim.

I stood there for a moment, hands on my knees, trying to get my breath while shooting daggers at Alex. I don't like being laughed at, and he seemed to think my training is all a big joke. He'd told me earlier that I didn't have the "martial arts mentality." I'd replied that I thought it was amazing that he could use three such big words in the same sentence and congratulated him on his improving verbal skills. So now he was a little sore at me. Hence the chuckling while Mr. Kim tossed me around like I was his own personal cat toy.

Speaking of Mr. Kim, he stood waiting for me to straighten up. I thought maybe a question would stall him before he sent me on another short flight across the room.

"Mr. Kim?" I said.

"Yes?"

"You told me that the only way to stop Simon Blankenship would be to find him first, right?"

"You are correct."

"Well, how are we going to do that? I mean, how are we going to find him when he has followers all over the world and a million places to hide and we never know where he is?"

Mr. Kim straightened his *do bak* and then, almost faster than I could see, he launched a spin kick. But this time I was ready, and since he was only going at about half speed, I was able to catch his kicking leg with my crossed arms and, at the same time, sweep his standing leg from under him with my foot and send him to the mat. Takedown, Rachel Buchanan! I couldn't believe I had done it. Soon I'd be starring in the remake of *Fists of Fury*. Hah! I gave Alex a smirk and was very pleased to see the look of total disbelief on his face. Brent smiled and gave me a big thumbs-up. He had a pretty cute smile when he smiled, which wasn't often.

"Excellent, Rachel! First rate!" Mr. Kim bounced back up quickly and beamed a big smile at me. "You showed excellent reflexes. Self-defense is a matter of planning ahead. When someone approaches you, someone who may be a potential foe, you must learn to subconsciously do a 'threat assessment.' If that person is an attacker, what are they likely to try first? From which direction might they launch a strike? Continually ask yourself those questions and eventually it will become second nature." Alex was shaking his head and staring at the floor.

Mr. Kim was still smiling. "How did you anticipate my kick?" he asked.

I paused for a moment and closed my eyes, replaying the sequence in my mind. I saw Mr. Kim straighten his *do bak* and then launch the kick. But wait. While he had straightened his uniform, his weight had shifted to his left leg as he prepared to kick with his right.

"I saw your weight shift right before you kicked. I knew something was coming, and it gave me a chance to prepare," I said.

"Excellent. You see what I mean? You can learn to do this almost without thinking, so you are always ready."

"Okay," I said, "but still, you were only at about half speed. If you'd been going full out, I never would have seen that kick coming," I said.

"Two things, Rachel. First, don't be negative. You did something well. Accept that. Second, you are correct, my skills in Tae Kwon Do far surpass yours at this point, but not everyone you meet in battle will have my level of skill. Most attackers are clumsy and unbalanced. In time, they will pose little threat to you. With enough study, you may reach Ninth Dan yourself."

Sure, and I also might open for Avril Lavigne. But he did have a point. Not the part about becoming Ninth Dan, but that in the last two months I had trained hard and I was getting better at this. To Alex's shock, I'd progressed all the way to a green belt. I mean, I'm still a klutz for the most part, but I was improving.

Wait a minute. Did he say "meet in battle"? *Battle?* Gulp.

Mr. Kim bowed and told me that the session was over for the day.

"Not so fast, mister," I said. "You still haven't answered my question. How are we going to find Blankenship?"

Mr. Kim smiled. "We will find him by letting him find us," he said. Huh?

"I'm sorry, is that some kind of Zen thing? I don't get it."

Mr. Kim laughed. I crack him up. (Most of the time.)

"There are two things Simon wants in this world. Since

we received his e-mail swearing vengeance on you, we know that one of those things is you. Can you guess what the other thing is?"

Mr. Kim is always doing that "answer a question with a question" thing. I hate that.

"Frequent-flyer miles?"

Mr. Kim chuckled again. "No, I'm sure free air travel is the least of Simon's worries. He needs the seven Mithrian treasures for his plan to work. If Simon can get his hands on those artifacts, he believes he will be able to summon the forces of Mithras and unleash them on the world. We have been working on the final translations in the *Book of Seraphim*. If we can decipher some of the riddles, we will know where to look for the relics. Then perhaps we can set a trap for Simon."

Setting traps sounded good. As long as the trap was like totally airtight and I was a long way away from the trap when it was sprung. Several states away from the trap, maybe.

"But if he somehow gets word that we've found a relic, something that's been missing for thousands of years, won't he be suspicious? Won't he try to set a trap for us instead?"

"Of course he will be wary. Simon is very intelligent and determined."

"Not to mention a total freak-a-zoid," I interrupted.

"Yes, that too. But he is also greedy and thirsting for power. That will make him careless. With the right circumstances and the right object, Simon should find himself unable to resist."

Alex and Brent stood there with their heads moving back and forth, watching us talk, like Mr. Kim and I were playing tennis.

"But what if we can't decipher the secrets of the book? Then what? We sit around and wait until somebody finds an artifact that we think he'll be interested in? That could take years," Alex said. Alex wasn't the patient type. In that respect I guess we were a bit alike.

"Remember, Alex, we must be cautious. Simon is a dangerous and deadly man. True, understanding the secrets of the book will not be easy. Scholars in Kuzbekistan have studied the book for years. And while many of the words have been translated, the meaning is often not clear. Our advantage is that it will be just as unclear to Simon and when we have what we need . . . "

Yada yada yada. He said some other stuff about how we must wait until the time is right and not be hasty and all that, but by then I had tuned him out. I'm a teenager, after all.

"I hate waiting," I said. Which was remarkably self-aware on my part, I thought. I'm absolutely no good at waiting. I open my birthday presents early. I'm first in line at the dessert table. I never wait for anything to go on sale.

"Yes, I've learned this about you. But perhaps something will happen sooner than you think." Mr. Kim bowed and dismissed me. I could swear that there was a twinkle in his eye. That meant he was up to something and he was keeping it to himself. So unfair! There was a lot of stuff that Mr. Kim hadn't explained to me yet. Each time I would start bugging him about the *Book of Seraphim*, he would change the subject. Or tell me that I "wasn't ready yet."

I couldn't stop thinking about that night on the ship. There had been a moment when we were trapped in the cargo hold, when I thought I saw . . . Well, I'm not sure what I saw. Someone or some*thing* standing in the smoke that was too horrible to imagine. Even now it gives me chills just thinking about it. At the time, since I was under a lot of stress, what with a real-life Dr. Evil trying to kill us and all, I figured it was my overactive imagination.

But later, when I told Mr. Kim about what I'd seen, he kind of freaked. And that alone was upsetting, because Mr. Kim doesn't freak about anything. It wasn't like he was scared. I don't think anything scares Mr. Kim, not even Simon Blankenship, who frankly scares the daylights out of me.

It was more like he got obsessed with what I thought I saw on the ship. He spent a lot of time asking me exactly what I'd seen, asking me to describe it and draw a picture of it. And he spent a lot of time running around the situation room looking at old dusty books and pulling up stuff on his computer and making all kinds of *tsk, tsk* sounds while he thought.

On the way back to my room, I kept running all this stuff over in my mind. Alex was trying to convince Brent that I had "just gotten lucky" in managing to knock down Mr. Kim, but as usual Brent wasn't talking too much. I tuned them out and thought instead about Simon trying to translate the book. My mind flashed to that thing that I saw in the smoke. It made me afraid that maybe Simon was getting some extra, otherworldly help. And that was scary in a lot of ways. At least he didn't have the real book. But I had this nagging feeling we didn't have much time before Simon made some kind of desperate move.

We reached the section of the school that splits off into the boys' and girls' wings. I waved good-bye to Alex and Brent and started toward my room.

"Hey, Raych?" It was Brent. I turned back to look at him. Alex had kept walking and was out of sight around the corner.

"Yeah?"

"I just wanted to tell you—you did really well this morning. You've improved a lot. You know how Alex likes to give you a hard time? It's all an act. He was impressed, and so was Mr. Kim. Just wanted you to know," he said. He stood there in the hallway looking all cute and Colin Farrell-y and tugging at his red *do bak* belt. For some reason I felt like blushing.

"Uh . . . thanks, Brent. Thank you," I said. As I've said, Brent was the shy, quiet type. But he had a way of saying the right things sometimes.

He nodded. "See you in Mic Elec," he said. He gave me a little mock salute, turned the corner, and was gone.

I headed to my room. One of the things I liked best about Blackthorn was my roommate, Pilar. We'd had a rocky start to our friendship. Most of it was my fault. I had a bit of an attitude when I got here. (Okay, sometimes I still do, ahem.)

As it turned out, Pilar has this odd psychic ability. Like, she gets feelings about stuff and most of the time her "feelings" turn out to be right. She started having weird dreams right after I got here—the *same* dream that *I* had the first night. And because she was getting all these weird vibes from me, she couldn't figure out if I could be trusted or if I was up to something. I can understand now how confusing it must have been. But since that night on the ship, she'd had no more dreams and we'd started to get along, with just a few little blips here and there.

One of those "blips" was her budding romance with Alex Scott. Pilar and Alex started dating before I got to Blackthorn. Although "dating" is not exactly the right word. Nobody ever actually goes anywhere at this school. Knowing Alex and Pilar, I bet most of their "dates" consisted of meeting at the gym so they could work out and get even more exercise. Or sitting in the school library and giving each other harder math problems.

Well, since Alex and I were like oil and water, this made things a little strained between Pilar and me sometimes. I thought Alex was a big jerk and he thought I was a troublemaker. I still wasn't sure what Pilar saw in him. I mean, yeah, Alex is cute. He's tall with short blond hair and cool, almost icy blue eyes. And he's buff. I've got to give her that.

And he does have this way of looking at you where he gets this kind of dreamy expression on his face. I mean, when he really turns it on, his eyes sparkle and he gets this sort of a half-smirk on his face that makes it seem like he knows what you're thinking. And he can be funny when he's not being a jerk. He's got a really deep voice and a nice laugh.

But aside from the eyes, the laugh, the buff-ness, and his overall cuteness, I really couldn't stand being around him. Not that I thought about it a lot or anything. Well, not very often. Just once in a while. Maybe.

When I got back to the room, Pilar was standing at the mirror, brushing her hair. Pilar is taller than me, and very slender. She has beautiful, curly, shoulder-length brown hair. I smiled to myself, thinking about how Pilar and I had gotten to be really good friends over the last couple of months. Confronting and defeating supervillains just naturally brings people closer, I guess.

Pilar was an orphan. Her mom died when she was young and an aunt raised her. Then her aunt got sick and couldn't care for her anymore, so Pilar ended up at Blackthorn. She had been here since she was twelve years old, and it was really the only stable home she'd ever had. In addition to her psychic "feelings," she was incredibly smart and thoughtful and really good at figuring things out.

A facsimile copy of the *Book of Seraphim* was lying open on her bed.

The *Book of Seraphim* is an ancient book that was written by Flavius, the last Emperor of Rome and a High Priest to Mithras. Mr. Kim and Simon Blankenship discovered the book in that Mithrian temple. This whole crazy mess started when Blankenship tried to steal the book from a gallery in Washington. I tried to steal the book back, except it got dropped in the river. We couldn't find it later, so Blankenship must have fished it out, but Mr. Kim says that because I tried so hard to get the book away from Simon, he'll believe it's the real one. Also, he's really ticked off at me for wrecking it. You know, in a wants-to-kill-us-all way.

Anyway, Flavius wrote the book as the Roman Empire was about to be overrun. He had lost a big battle to forces from the Persian Empire who worshiped the goddess Etherea. (Sometimes I needed a scorecard to keep all the different empires, gods, and goddesses straight.) Mr. Kim only told us a little about what's in the book, but it's supposed to tell how followers of Mithras can find some hidden relics, do a bunch of chanting and dancing around, and bring Mithras back to life when the time is right. Mithras, if I forgot to mention it, was the Roman god of Darkness and the Afterlife. The Romans believed that worshiping Mithras would make their armies invincible. Unfortunately the Persians that gave the Romans a major butt-kicking didn't know they were supposed to lose. So Mithras was banished to the underworld by Etherea, the Goddess of Light.

Mr. Kim had given Pilar a copy of the pages of the real book, and she spent all of her free time studying them. There were several hundred pages in the book, and she spent a couple of hours every night going through it. It was an obsession. It was more than an obsession. Figuring out the secrets of that book had almost become her sole reason for being. Is there a word for something beyond obsession? That is what that book was to Pilar.

I thought all of this sounded like a big load of mystical hooey. I know that people worship all kinds of stuff, but this just seemed too out there. Simon Blankenship as Mithras, and me as Etherea—talk about being a few fries short of a Happy Meal! I mean, if I really was a goddess, I'm sure I'd have better hair.

"I hate my hair," Pilar said.

"I *love* your hair," I said. Watching her run a brush through her hair every morning was agonizing to someone as hair-challenged as myself.

"You say that every morning."

"It's true every morning. I'd kill for hair like that." Since

Pilar and Alex had started getting closer, she spent a lot more time on her hair. Gag.

Pilar finished brushing and sat down at her desk. "How was your lesson?" she asked.

"Time passes quickly when you're flying though the air. But I did manage one take-down on Mr. Kim."

"No way!" Her eyes went wide in astonishment.

"Way. He was only going at about half speed, but I still managed to block his kick and bring him down with a front sweep. Went totally Power Rangers on his butt."

Pilar looked impressed. She had just gotten her red belt with a black stripe, three ranks higher than me. She'd be testing for her black belt in a few months.

"It sounds like all the extra work is paying off," she said.

"Yep." I took off my *do bak* and threw on my robe. I needed to hit the shower before breakfast. Lately showers were taking me longer because I needed to soak the bumps and bruises out of me. But that's the price you pay when a madman is pursuing you.

"Raych?" Pilar said. "Are you afraid?"

"Of what?"

"Mithras. Blankenship. Whatever you want to call him."

She had a worried look on her face. Pilar is probably the smartest person I've ever met, next to maybe Mr. Kim, but I've learned that she's also incredibly sensitive. Things tend to bother her more than other people.

"Sometimes, I guess. I try not to think about it. I figure Blankenship is just a crazy crook and those guys usually slip up and get caught. Why?" I wasn't telling the whole truth here. I thought about it a lot. But Pilar didn't need to know that. Although she *was* psychic, so she probably already knew it.

"I don't know. I just wondered, I guess."

She still looked troubled.

"Come on. Spill it. What's bothering you?" I said.

"I started having dreams again," she said. I willed the blood not to drain from my face. To be perfectly honest, her dreams kind of freaked me out a little. Okay, they freaked me out a lot.

"Go on," I said in my most reassuring, "I'm completely unconcerned" tone.

"I keep seeing you dressed in white robes and floating in the air. Then you start falling and none of us can catch you and you keep falling toward Mithras and then he changes into a bull and just as you're about to land on his horns, I wake up."

"Wait a minute. Did you say that I'm wearing white robes in the dream?" I asked.

"Yes, why?"

"Well, white isn't really my color. I'm more of an autumn. Do you think next time you could dream me in something with earth tones?"

"Stop joking, Rachel. This guy is dangerous. I don't want anything to happen to you!"

"Pilar, look, I know that Blankenship is crazy and dangerous, probably better than anyone. But we aren't exactly shooting blanks at him. Mr. Kim and the FBI agents are all pretty smart people. Plus, I think we're safe here at Blackthorn. So you don't need to worry."

Pilar seemed relieved.

"Well, I hope not. Look, I've got to run. I'm meeting Alex before breakfast, so he can help me with my Cultures paper," she said. "See you at breakfast?"

"Alex again?" I snorted.

Her face colored slightly.

"I know how you feel about Alex, Rachel, but you don't know him like I do. He's really very sweet."

Alex sweet? I think I'm nauseous now.

I didn't feel like an argument so early in the morning, so I shrugged and she left the room. I thought it was cool that Pilar was worried about me. I still wasn't sure how much I believed in all that psychic stuff, but after seeing so much of it firsthand, I had to think it was possible. Heck, I'd just met a guy who thought he was the living incarnation of a Roman god. If Pilar being a psychic was crazy, it was way down on the list from that. So I should take her dreams seriously.

Still, I didn't want her to worry. Mr. Kim had my back, and so did Agent Tyler and the FBI. I felt perfectly safe as long as I was at Blackthorn. Blankenship and his bull people couldn't touch me here.

If only I'd stayed put.

CHAPTER TWO

The Great Escape

The next night we met in THE BIG SECRET SPY ROOM THAT'S HIDDEN UNDER THE SCHOOL AND ACCESSIBLE ONLY BY SECRET PASSAGE FROM MR. KIM'S OFFICE. For weeks I had tried to come up with a really cool name for this place. All the good names like Bat Cave and Fortress of Solitude were already taken, and nothing else I could think of would do it justice. So I had started referring to it as THE BIG SECRET SPY ROOM THAT'S HIDDEN UNDER THE SCHOOL AND ACCESSIBLE ONLY BY SECRET PASSAGE FROM MR. KIM'S OFFICE. Wordy, but it would have to do for now.

Mr. Kim had us here almost every night for an hour or so to talk about the case. We were trying to figure out where Mithras might strike next. Mostly I sat there and drooled over the computers and lab equipment and other high-tech gadgets. The best part is that Mr. Kim had started to give us some really cool stuff of our own.

After our first encounter with Mithras, Mr. Kim had special electrical circuits installed in our rooms so that when he wanted to see us, the desk lamps on our desks would blink on and off. We also got panic buttons in our bedrooms that we could push to summon school security if we needed to. And these *really* cool watches with miniature cell-phone transmitters in them so we could communicate with one another. If Mr. Kim needed us when we were out of our rooms, the watches would silently vibrate. Then we could find a quiet place and actually speak into the watch to talk with Mr. Kim or Agent Tyler.

We had to be careful no one saw us using this stuff, though. Not even the Top Floor students had keen gear like us. So that was way cool, being the only students at the school who knew the real truth about Blackthorn Academy.

THE BIG SECRET SPY ROOM THAT'S HIDDEN UNDER THE SCHOOL AND ACCESSIBLE ONLY BY SECRET PASSAGE FROM MR. KIM'S OFFICE held enough lab equipment, computers, satellite phones, DNA analyzers, and spy stuff to launch an invasion of a small country. Blackthorn Academy was built into the side of a mountain, and this room was about ten stories below the school, carved out of a giant cave in the mountainside. In the center of the room was a conference table with a four-sided video monitor in the middle of it. Here Mr. Kim could call up FBI or CIA stations all over the world.

On this night he sat there talking with Mr. Quinn, the

Criminology and Abnormal Psychology instructor. Mr. Quinn also attended Blackthorn Academy. He was a major brainiac who pretty much invented the FBI's National Crime Index when he was still a student here. He taught full-time at Blackthorn because he loved the school, but he also consulted with the FBI and helped them to develop psychological profiles of criminals.

Mr. Quinn and Mr. Kim sat on the ends of the conference table and I sat next to Brent. He asked me if he could take my watch off my wrist for a minute, and I nodded as he gently removed it. He took the back of the watch off with a tiny screwdriver and fiddled around inside it. Pilar and Alex sat next to each other on the other side of the table. Every so often Pilar would look up at Alex with this big old moony-eyed expression and he would smile back at her and then she'd blush and look back at her copy of the book. May I say: ewwww.

Since they were making me nauseous, I watched Brent poke around the inside of the watch instead. Brent was pretty smart about gadgets and machines and stuff like that. He was in my Mic Elec class and he was easily the smartest student in the room. He could fix anything electrical or mechanical, and he was always taking different parts of stuff and making little gizmos. None of us had the slightest idea what they did.

"What are you doing?" I asked him.

"Fixing your watch," he said.

"What? Is it broken already?" Mr. Kim had just given them to us a few weeks ago.

"Nope," he said. He didn't look up at me or say anything

more than that. He was the quiet, mysterious type. But I had also noticed that when Brent *did* say something, it was usually something smart and important.

For some reason I couldn't concentrate tonight. Maybe it was Pilar telling me her dream that had me spooked, but I felt jumpy and out of sorts.

"So," Mr. Kim said. "Does anyone have any ideas or thoughts?"

"Yeah," I said. "I think we need to find the rest of the missing artifacts before Simon does." I like to cut right to the important stuff.

Alex slapped his forehead with his hand. Then he got that smirky expression he always gets.

"I don't know why *we* didn't think of that," he said. "You really are *brilliant*."

I shot him the hairy eyeball, but it just made him smirkier.

"Look," I said, "we've gone over what happened on the ship about a million times. So I think we need to start with the artifacts themselves. What do we know about them?"

Mr. Quinn ran it down for us, tapping a keyboard in front of him.

"According to the early translations of the book, there are seven artifacts," he said.

Drawings of some old-looking stuff popped onto the video monitor.

"These are artist's renderings of the four remaining missing Mithrian Relics, based on their description in the book. The first is the Clawhorn Chalice." The image showed a big silver cup with what looked like an eagle's claw or some other giant bird foot holding up the cup part. It had a lot of jewels in it and the carving of a bull's head in the base. "Next is the Scepter of Light." This was a long golden pointy thing that looked like a baseball bat, with more jewels stuck in it. "The Idol of Fury." It was a large golden statue of a bull sitting on its hindquarters, covered with jewels. Obviously there was a bling bling theme here. "And finally, the Lance of Mithras." The final drawing showed a big spear that was made out of some type of shiny metal with—you guessed it—a lot of rubies and emeralds in the shaft.

Mr. Quinn went on. "Emperor Flavius had these items hidden when he was losing control of the Empire. According to the book, the Seven Relics were blessed by Mithras. They must be found and brought together in order to bring Mithras back to life in this world."

"What about the other three objects?" asked Alex.

"We know Simon has the Medallion of Truth. You saw him wearing it on the ship. That was stolen from a museum in Greece many years ago. The Scroll of the Enlightened is in a museum in Kuzbekistan. The other is the Firehorn. It was discovered years ago in Africa and is currently in the home of a wealthy collector in Los Angeles."

"But wait," I said. "If these dusty old things are so valuable, why don't we take them out of the museum and get them from the collector and hide them somewhere that Mithras can never find them?"

"Easier said than done, Rachel," Mr. Kim said. "First,

Kuzbekistan is a very unstable country. Its government is quite protective of its artifacts. As for the collector, he refuses to give up the piece and insists he can safeguard it. For all we know, Simon may be controlling these governments and individuals to keep the relics safe until he needs them. It is only by luck that Simon was not able to get the genuine *Book of Seraphim* out of Kuzbekistan. The decision to send the book to this country for display was nearly a disaster."

"So what do we do now?" I said.

"Pilar, you have read through most of the book," Mr. Kim said. "Do you have any ideas?"

"Not so far," she said. "It doesn't make a lot of sense. Assuming the translations are accurate, Flavius sent seven of his most trusted Centurions away, each of them with one of the pieces. None of them knew where any of the others were going. They were to sail to these destinations and build a temple to keep the artifact safe. But each destination is like a big riddle. I can't figure them out."

Mr. Kim nodded. He walked over to the small vault where he kept the authentic book, protected by a handprint scanner and a combination, and brought the book carefully back to the table. It was a beautiful thing. The front was covered in jewels, except in the very middle, where there was a clasp that must have held a giant gem of some kind, now missing. Mr. Kim thought that maybe someone had stolen it from the temple. From that center clasp, a line of small diamonds radiated out from the center to where each line ended at a pretty good-size ruby. It looked like the center stone was the sun and each of these lines of diamonds that led to the sapphire were the rays of the sun radiating out from the center. It was pretty cool-looking.

"So far we haven't had any luck either," said Mr. Kim. He stared at the book like maybe if he studied it long enough a clue would magically appear.

"Just out of curiosity," I said, "where were the Medallion, the Firehorn, and the Scroll discovered?"

Mr. Quinn hit his keyboard and a world map popped up on the screen. He highlighted the area where each artifact was discovered with a little blue dot. There was a blue dot on the western coast of India, one on a little island off the coast of Greece, and one on the west coast of Africa. When I looked at those little dots, something started working in my brain. After a moment I asked Mr. Kim to put a dot on where the Book had been found in Kuzbekistan. Somehow something about the way they were all laid out on the map was familiar. It was like it was right on the tip of my tongue or the edges of my vision. But I couldn't quite place it.

I pulled the book in front of me and very carefully opened it up. The endpapers of the book were made of thick parchment. On one endpaper was a drawing of a world map as it existed in the time of the Emperor Flavius, with a lot of empty space off in the oceans and stuff.

Something about those blue dots was tugging at my brain.

"Pilar, these words around the edges of the map—what do they say?" I asked.

"You got me. They seem to be little prayers or devotions to

Mithras or something." She pointed to the one on the far edge of the map. "This one says 'Mithras walks with Hades' handmaiden.' This one says 'Mithras shall thunder from the mountain.' They're totally random and don't make any sense that I can see."

I studied the map for a moment and then it hit me. I knew. I knew what had been bugging me about the pattern I'd seen earlier.

"Mr. Quinn, can you scan this map from the book into the computer?"

He looked at Mr. Kim, who nodded.

"Then that world map you have that shows where the artifacts were discovered? Is there some way you can adjust both of these maps so that the scale measurement is the same for each?"

"Well, yes, but it won't be exact. The map from the book is hand drawn and the map I'm using is from a satellite image. It won't make a perfect—"

I interrupted him, because Mr. Quinn, smart as he is, has a tendency to prattle on sometimes. And they say teenagers have a hard time staying on task.

"I understand. Just try to make as close a match as you can," I said.

He went to work on the computer and his fingers flew over the keyboard. We watched the screen, and the cursor on the screen was flying all around like some kind of Frisbee on steroids. Lines appeared and little icons circled the edges of both maps. Then both maps appeared on the screen side by side.

"There. The calibration is as close to scale as I can get it," he said.

"Okay, now, can you scale the today map down so that when it prints out from the screen it will be the exact same size as the cover of the book? And can you print it out with all of the blue dots on it?"

Mr. Quinn looked at me quizzically but pulled a ruler from the drawer at the table and measured the dimensions of the book.

"What are you doing?" Alex said.

"I'm not sure, just an idea," I said.

The *Book of Seraphim* was a big oversized book, with the binding on the short side of the rectangle, sort of like an old-fashioned scrapbook or something. I took the map from Mr. Quinn and oriented it so it matched the layout of the cover. When I laid the map on top of the cover, a very strange thing happened.

Each blue dot where one of the artifacts had been found lined up perfectly with one of the giant rubies on the cover of the book. And the blue dot on the map that represented where the book had been found was directly over the center spot where the missing gemstone should have been. It was a perfect match. I had to give a shout-out to Flavius, because he had used the oldest trick there was. He had hidden the map to the artifacts in plain sight.

"Well," I said. "At least now I think we know where to look."

CHAPTER THREE

I Rule. Oh Yes I Do.

No one said anything for a minute.

Alex, who usually gets all smart-alecky at a time like this, was the first one to say something.

"Could it really be that simple?" he said. Wow. Not even a zinger. Alex must be really stunned.

"Why not?" I said. "Think about it. The other night Pilar read to me the final section of the book, where Flavius sends his men out to hide the artifacts. It sounded like he knew it was over for him and he wanted them all to be scattered around the world so that they'd be safe from Etherea."

"Sure, but—" Alex started to interrupt me.

"But when I saw the map Mr. Quinn put up on the screen, the one where the artifacts we know about were discovered, something bugged me about it. The way they were laid out was like a pattern or something. Flavius knew where each Centurion was going. But no one else knew. So just to make sure there was a record, he made sure the rubies matched up. Little clues just as a fail-safe."

"But if this map is correct, then some of these artifacts are hidden in places that the Romans couldn't have even known existed. How is that possible?" he said.

Right then, I had a flashback to the night on the boat when I saw that thing. A horrible, hideous, man-bull thing that had screamed with an otherworldly fury. Something could have helped Flavius. I knew that I was right. And if this map was correct, we'd find the other artifacts hidden in England, Hawaii, South America, and Japan. Sure, those were all big places, but at the very least it gave us somewhere to start.

"Look," I said. "I don't know how all this happened. But we know that we're dealing with something weird here—mystical forces and ancient gods and probably the Force from *Star Wars*, for all I know. These artifacts are there. I know it like I know my own name."

Mr. Kim looked at me with a curious expression. He almost smiled. Like he was proud of me or something.

"There's a problem, though," Pilar said. "Even if this is right, we're still talking about thousands of square miles. I mean, Japan, England—even the Big Island of Hawaii is like four thousand square miles or something. How will we know where to look?"

Because I am a teenager and in possession of a teenage

brain, and even though I was in the middle of a very serious, potentially deadly situation, I paused for a moment to reflect on how incredibly geeky it was that Pilar happened to know the square mileage of the Big Island of Hawaii. If we ever got Blankenship behind bars, I was taking all three of these guys to the nearest shopping mall to get them an iPod and a copy of *Entertainment Weekly*.

"I'm way ahead of you," I said. "Mr. Quinn, can you run an Internet search, maybe through some archaeological sites, and find out if any of these places have ever had discoveries of Roman artifacts or settlements? I mean, I know England will, because on the day I stayed awake in history class I vaguely remember the teacher saying that there were Romans there, but what about the other places?"

Mr. Quinn leaned back in his chair for a minute and stared up at the ceiling. You could almost see the microchips firing in his brain. He held that pose for several moments, then leaned forward and his fingers started flying over the keyboard. For a second I had a really bad case of keyboard envy. Gosh, I missed the Internet.

"I don't believe it," he said finally.

"Both Hawaii and Japan have turned up Roman-era artifacts. Of course, England is overrun with sites; everyone knows the Roman Empire extended that far. But there is also evidence of Roman presence in early feudal Japan. And in 1954 at a dig site near Hilo, on the Big Island of Hawaii, archaeologists uncovered a helmet and a few pieces of armor that were confirmed to be of Roman origin. It was a major discovery at the time.

"Scientists speculated that a Roman ship became lost in the South Pacific and was either shipwrecked there or else lost at sea and the wreckage washed up on the island. The site is still being excavated to this day, and a few pieces have been found on other islands, probably traded or carried there by natives who discovered or met up with the Roman survivors . . . assuming there were survivors.

"The story is almost the same in Japan. A site in northern Japan was discovered in the 1920s. Roman helmets, swords, and other items. Same conclusion by the archaeologists: a ship that got lost or perhaps Roman soldiers taken captive by Chinese or Korean warriors."

Alex was still unconvinced. Paging Dr. Skeptical! Please report to the ER, stat!

"It just seems so unlikely that they could have gotten that far from Rome," he said.

"Not necessarily," said Mr. Quinn. "Remember, the Mongols invaded overland from China all the way to Europe. So Europeans moving in the other direction is certainly possible," he said.

"So that's it," I said. "That's where we start."

"Well, let's not be hasty," Mr. Kim said. "This is certainly food for thought, but I think we need to study it further before we investigate."

"I've always wanted to go to Japan. I hear they have good sushi and karaoke there. I love sushi," I said, choosing to ignore him.

"Rachel, even if you are correct, you won't be going anywhere except to your classes. If Mr. Quinn and I determine further action is necessary, we will be the ones to investigate. We can't risk exposing you to Simon again. It would be too dangerous."

"Maybe we should start in Hawaii. We could breeze in, find the treasure, work on our tans, and maybe catch a luau," I said, still ignoring him. "A little sun would be good for all of us."

Mr. Kim smiled and shook his head.

"Rachel, you don't have the necessary training." And more of the blah, blah, blah about what I didn't have.

I decided to try a different approach.

"Okay. If you don't want our help finding this stuff, that's fine." Yeah, right. "But I think you better get started right away. Like tonight," I said.

"Rachel, patience is a virtue." Mr. Kim laughed.

"Listen to me. You replaced the *Book of Seraphim* with a copy, so the one that Simon stole is a fake, right?"

"Correct," said Mr. Kim.

"How accurate a forgery is it?" I said.

"It is a very careful forgery. Changes were made in the text in subtle ways so that a cursory comparison won't show any differences. But the appearance and the design of the forged book are identical to the authentic one. Right down to the missing gem on the cover," he said.

"That's what I was afraid of," I said.

"Why?" said Mr. Kim.

"Because," I said, trying to sound all nonchalant, like I really wasn't that interested unless he changed his mind and gave us the trips to Hawaii and Japan that we so totally deserved, "it means that if *we* have this map of the gems, from right on the cover of the book, then so does Simon. Remember? You said the cover was identical to his copy. He might not figure it out . . . but what if he does?"

Mr. Kim went speechless for a moment and the color drained from his face. Then he looked at Mr. Quinn.

"Oops," he said.

CHAPTER FOUR

I Prove Invaluable to the Cause

Even though I had this moment of brilliance and everything, Mr. Kim and Mr. Quinn still wouldn't let us come. The next night in THE BIG SECRET SPY ROOM THAT'S HIDDEN UNDER THE SCHOOL AND ACCESSIBLE ONLY BY SECRET PASSAGE FROM MR. KIM'S OFFICE, Mr. Kim explained that he and Mr. Quinn were going to Oahu to investigate. Well, I said boo on that. They were going to tell Mrs. Marquardt and Mr. Torres that they were going to an educational conference and leave them in charge of the school. Double boo. Leaving Mrs. Marquardt in charge? I was very pouty while Mr. Kim delivered the news.

"There is something I have to tell you all," said Mr. Kim. He sounded serious, so we all stopped fidgeting and sat up in our seats.

"You need to understand how dangerous this is. Simon Blankenship is an evil man. He wouldn't hesitate for a moment to harm any of you. I want it to be perfectly clear that you are not to do anything reckless or foolish while Mr. Quinn and I are gone." He was looking at me when he said the reckless and foolish part. Why does he always look at me when he says that kind of stuff? I am so totally not reckless and foolish! As if.

"Secondly, you need to realize that Simon has vast resources. He has a dedicated and fanatical group of followers. My point is that, under the circumstances, you can trust no one. Only the six of us in this room know that we have the authentic book. No matter what happens, that book must not fall into Simon's hands." Mr. Kim looked at all of us, one by one. "Above all else, you must remember that Simon's people could be anywhere. So act accordingly. Trust no one.

"While we're gone, I think it would be a good idea if the four of you continue to meet here. You may work on trying to unravel the secrets of the book," he said.

"That's it? That's your idea of us helping to catch Mithras?" I said. "I'm sorry. For a minute there I might have dozed off because it sounded *so* boring! Fine. Go jetting off to Hawaii or wherever and have the secret-agent fun. We'll just stay here and be bored out of our skulls. No problemo!"

He said it like it was a big honor. Like we should be thrilled that we were free to come and go in THE BIG SECRET SPY ROOM THAT'S HIDDEN UNDER THE SCHOOL AND ACCESSIBLE ONLY BY SECRET PASSAGE FROM MR. KIM'S OFFICE, even if he wasn't around. Personally, I thought he was crazy. Who knew how much trouble we could get into with all this stuff down here? But I kept that thought to myself.

"We'll be gone a few days," he said, ignoring my tirade. "Try not to get yourself into any dangerous situations while we're gone." Again he looked at me. I think Mr. Kim was starting to have "trust issues" where I was concerned.

"Do you want us to dust and vacuum while you're gone?" I said as they loaded the car. I didn't even try to keep the sarcasm out of my voice.

"Now that you mention it, this room could use a good dusting," Mr. Kim said.

They both laughed and then got in the car and drove away.

Well, I had news for them. Rachel Buchanan does not do anyone's dusting. Especially someone who tries to keep her from her free trip to Hawaii.

CHAPTER FIVE

No One Is Going to Cheat Me Out of My Hula Lessons

"This is so infuriating," I said. "He told me we'd get to help bring this knucklehead down, and then they take off for who knows where and leave us behind?" I was working up a full head of Rachel Buchanan steam, and my friends had seen enough of it to back off and let me rant.

We sat in THE BIG SECRET . . . oh forget it . . . the room for a couple of hours while I worked on a full-blown meltdown at the injustice of my life.

I kept pacing back and forth and yammering on and on about how unfair everything was. In the meantime, Brent kept fiddling with my watch, Alex just sat there flexing his muscles, and Pilar did something with the computer. None of them seemed to realize the seriousness of our situation, which was that we were stuck here at school when we could be in Hawaii or some other exotic locale. I mean, come on. Focus, people!

Finally, as usual, Alex spoke up, if only to needle me.

"When do you want to get started on that dusting?" he said.

"Very funny," I said. Then I noticed that Pilar was looking at the computer screen and frowning.

"What?" I said to her.

She had one of those looks on her face. That "something is going on here and I know something the rest of you don't and it's really bugging me" look.

She glanced up at me.

"Ummm, nothing . . . ," she said.

"Pilar," I said. "Spill it."

"Really, it's nothing," she said.

"Okay. You of all people should know better by now. We can sit here and do this all night. I'll say 'Pilar, what's on your mind?' and you'll say 'Oh, nothing' and it will go on like that for hours until I finally drag it out of you. So let's save time and you just tell me."

Pilar punched a few buttons on the keyboard and the big-screen monitor on the wall brought up an image of an archaeological dig site.

"This is the site on the Big Island, where the first Roman artifacts were found. Shields, swords, that kind of stuff," she said.

"Yes?" I said.

"Well, I know Mr. Quinn said some Roman-era stuff was found on the other islands, which is why they're starting on

Oahu, but this is where it was found first, and I think it's important," she said.

Good heavens. This was going to take *days*! Even Alex and Brent were paying attention to her now.

"It's just one phrase in the book—I keep thinking about it," she said. "It says 'Mithras walks with Hades' handmaiden.' It didn't make any sense to me at first. But now something's telling me it's connected to this. I can't explain it."

She clicked through some pictures of the dig site. I watched as the images moved by on the screen. Then I saw something. Something that made my flesh crawl.

"Wait! Pilar, go back to that last picture!"

Pilar punched the keyboard and the previous image came up.

"I think you're right," I said. "This is the place to start."

"Why are you always so sure that you're . . . ," Alex started to say, but I shushed him. I picked up a little laser pointer that was lying on the table and pointed it at the monitor up on the wall.

"Because of this," I said. I moved the red dot of the pointer to the bottom right corner of the photograph. An archaeologist was standing next to a rock wall, holding an old bronze helmet that must have belonged to a Roman soldier. Behind him, on the wall of rock down close to the ground, where I'd almost missed it, was a carving in the stone.

A carving of a bull's head.

CHAPTER SIX

Holy Cow!

"Holy cow!" said Brent.

"I think that nails it. The Romans made it to that island alive," I said.

Alex had that stunned expression on his face, like he wasn't quite ready to give in.

"Okay, I'll admit that it looks like the carvings that Simon has on all of his stuff. But even if this is all true, how do we know the artifact is still there? Maybe someone found it and carried it off."

"It's there," said Pilar.

"How do you know?" he said.

"Because I know," she said.

Alex didn't say anything, clearly not wanting to get into that argument again. I may think he's a jerk, and he's clearly uncomfortable with Pilar's gifts, but at least he tried not to hurt her feelings. I gave him props for that.

Pilar's announcement sealed it for me, though. I mean, sure, a ton of circumstantial evidence and a wacky feeling from my roommate was all I really had to go on. But I didn't need a lot of convincing. I'm easy that way. Especially if it's going to get me to Hawaii.

"What do we do?" Brent asked.

"They're on a plane by now. They said they're going to Oahu, but we have no idea where, or how to get in touch with them," Alex said.

All true. We had no way of getting this info to them. They didn't even give us their cell-phone numbers, because they were worried about Mithrians listening in. Who knew how much time they'd waste wandering around Oahu when they really needed to be on the Big Island.

"Maybe Mrs. Marquardt knows how to get in touch with him?" Alex said.

"And what do we tell her that would possibly convince her to interrupt him at his 'conference,' without spilling the beans?" I said.

They nodded. I felt like a clock was ticking in my head and we were running out of time.

"Okay. So we need to get out of here and start working on finding those artifacts. Are you guys in?"

Pilar, Brent, and Alex all looked at one another. They weren't like me. (At least not yet.) They were superloyal to Mr. Kim, and I could tell that their first instinct was to tell me we should stay at the school and mind our own beeswax. But they'd also gotten a glimpse of what was at stake on the ship that night. They knew that Simon needed to be stopped. So, they were torn. Time for some of the old Rachel charm.

"Guys, look, I know what you're thinking. You want to obey Mr. Kim's orders and stay out of it. But Mr. Kim is not infallible. Correct me if I'm wrong, but whose idea was it to give Simon a copy of the book that ends up having directions to the treasures right on the front cover? We should be putting all the resources we have into catching Simon and finding these little gizmos. And *we* are resources, aren't we?" They all nodded. Except for maybe Alex. I couldn't tell if he nodded or not. Alex was something of a stick-in-the-mud when it came to bending the rules. Once he got past the actual rule-breaking he was fine, but it was the part leading up to the act that he had trouble with.

"So it's a waste of resources for us to sit here and do nothing, right?" I said.

"I guess so," Pilar said.

"I suppose," said Alex. Even when he knew I was right, he couldn't give me an inch.

Brent, Mr. Verbose, just nodded in agreement. Never use two nods when one will do.

"Then the first thing we need to do is figure out how to get out of school without Mrs. Marquardt catching on," I said.

"You can't be serious," Pilar said.

"I'm totally serious."

"Rachel, come on, this is not like heading to Washington, D.C. in a van. We're talking about Hawaii. Even if we could leave the school, we don't have any way to get there."

"One step at a time. Alex, think about this. We have to get past Mrs. Marquardt. That's our tactical objective. How do we do it?" I said.

I had noticed that Alex was good at this kind of thing. If I could get him to focus on a profect by putting it all into macho-military-type terms, he wouldn't be such a whiner about breaking the rules.

"Look," he said. "If we go charging in like this again, Mr. Kim could decide enough is enough and throw us all out of here. And then what? We all move back to Beverly Hills with you?"

This was taking a little longer than I thought. The guy sure was thickheaded.

"Fine, if you're not up to the task, we'll just . . ." I said. That did it.

"I didn't say I wasn't up to the task! Oh, you make me so mad sometimes. Wait here."

Alex stalked over to one of the computers and sat down. Soon he came back with a piece of paper in his hand.

Alex had gone on the FBI website and downloaded their logo onto the page to make it look like an official FBI letter-head from Special Agent Nathan Tyler, with a letter to Mr. Kim. It said that Tyler was more than happy to make arrangements for Alex Scott, Brent Christian, Rachel Buchanan, and Pilar Jordan to attend the weeklong Introduction to FBI Careers Camp at Quantico. The letter said we'd be attending the camp starting tomorrow for the next week, and that he would arrange for FBI transportation to pick us up at school in the morning. It had all the right dates and just the right tone, and it sounded totally official. Alex took a stack of fax pages out of the incoming tray of the fax machine. He sorted through them, found a letter that Agent Tyler had faxed to Mr. Kim, and traced over Agent Tyler's signature. It was a really good forgery.

"You realize this is probably a huge felony. Impersonating an FBI agent or something," I said. I wanted to make sure he wasn't the only one that was aware of all the rules.

"I'm not impersonating an agent," he said. "I'm impersonating an agent's letter. Besides, if we get caught, you'll be in so much more trouble as the ringleader of this little operation that I'll just be an afterthought."

Right, I thought. *That'll hold up in court. Ringleader? Me?*

"We need one more thing," Alex said as he sat back down at the computer. He typed out a note from Mr. Kim to Mrs. Marquardt.

> Mrs. Marquardt:
>
> In my rush to leave for the conference, I neglected to inform you that Rachel, Alex, Pilar, and Brent will be attending a special FBI Careers Camp at Quantico for the next few days as guests of Agent Tyler. He has arranged their transportation and they will be picked up here on Wednesday. You can reach me on my cell phone with any questions.
>
> Thanks,
>
> *Jonathon Kim*

"She's never going to buy this," I said.

"Yes, she will. We'll leave it in a file folder in the box outside her office door tonight, like Mr. Kim put it there before he left. If we show up in the morning with our bags packed, she won't think twice. Brent and I will load up the Henderson's Dry Cleaning Van and park it out in the woods tonight. We'll hustle out the front door, circle around the school, and hop in the van. Then we're gone."

Pilar asked good questions as usual. "That's great, but that only gets us out of school. We can't drive the van to Hawaii."

They all looked at me like they expected me to do something. Like it was my job to come up with this part of the scheme. *Think, Rachel.*

"Wait here," I said. I ran back up the stairs. Okay, jogged back up the stairs. Well, walked really quickly. I mean, I knew time was of the essence, but it is like ten flights of stairs already. I got to my room, grabbed my laptop, and hurried back down to the hideout. I plugged the computer into one of the Ethernet connections and went to the website for Buchanan Enterprises of Beverly Hills.

"What are you doing?" Brent asked.

"She's getting us a ride to Hawaii," Pilar said. See what I mean? Sometimes she just knows what I'm up to. It's kind of neat and creepy all at once.

I think I've said before that I'm pretty good with computers. One night, after I'd come home late, I noticed that my dad had left his computer on in his study, still logged in to his office network. So of course I sat down and had a couple hours of fun.

I was able to get into the protocols, find my dad's password, and read his e-mail. *Oh so boring.* But since the computer thought I was Charles Buchanan, I was also able to set up a few little "trapdoors" on the company website.

I created a little program that I transferred to a file on my laptop that enabled me to get into the Buchanan Enterprises system. It was set up so that the company network thought I was my dad logging on from a remote location. It got me right past the security and I could do whatever I wanted. All I needed to do was go to the search engine on the website and type in "charlesisabigdoofus."

I never did anything destructive like some hackers. Mainly I just wanted to see if I could do it. I figured if I got caught, Dad would just think I was acting out again and I'd get grounded or something, as usual.

"Great. But how does that help us?" asked Alex after I explained what I was doing.

"She's going to order us an airplane," Pilar said.

My roomie the psychic. Once this was all over, we should get her a TV show, a website, and a 900 number and start raking in the cash.

I went into the Buchanan Enterprises network through my trapdoor. In a few minutes I found the company travel department. From there I was able to pull up a list of charter air services that used the Philadelphia airport. I scanned through the list of possibilities until I found one that looked promising. Hopefully there would still be someone answering the phone at this time of night.

"Hansen Charter Jet Service," a voice said. Whew.

"Hello, my name is Theresa Barnett." (Theresa was my dad's secretary.) "I'm calling from Buchanan Enterprises in Beverly Hills," I said. Pilar, Alex, and Brent were staring at me with their mouths open.

I explained that I was calling to arrange a charter flight to Hawaii for Mr. Buchanan's daughter and a few of her classmates to attend a special environmental workshop on marine mammals. "Mr. Buchanan's daughter is very interested in saving the whales, you see. I'd like to know if we could arrange a flight from Philadelphia to Hilo, Hawaii, through your service."

After some discussion, I was able to arrange a charter flight on a small executive jet from Philadelphia to Hilo for $8,000. Score!

"Thank you so very much for your help. You may bill the charges directly to the company Platinum American Express. I'll be sure to tell Mr. Buchanan how helpful you were in arranging this for his beloved daughter, and Buchanan Enterprises will be sure to use Hansen Charter Jet Service for all of our future air charter needs." There are definitely advantages to having a rich and powerful father.

When I hung up the phone, I was shaking. Charles was going to freak when he found out what I did. But I'd worry about that later. I used the travel service to book online reservations for two rooms in a Hilo hotel. Then I backed out of the system through my trapdoor, and logged off the website.

Pilar and the boys were looking at me with stunned expressions.

"Holy . . . What the heck did you just do?" Alex said.

"She did what needed to be done," said Pilar. "Just like last time."

"She just committed about sixteen felonies is what she did," Alex said. "Do you realize how much trouble we'll be in if we go through with this?" Now all of sudden Alex was back to being Mr. Big Fraidy Cat.

"I don't care. If one of you wants out, tell me now. But if you're in, say so. Brent, you can just nod."

Brent nodded right away. Pilar gave me the thumbs-up. Alex was back into his teenage macho act, and he clearly didn't like my implication that he was being a wuss, but after a moment he mumbled his agreement as well.

"Okay. We have work to do. We need to be at Mrs. Marquardt's office at seven-thirty in the morning. The flight is scheduled for nine-thirty departure. Alex and Brent, you guys get the van ready. Brent, make sure you get a cell phone for each of us from the equipment locker, plus anything else you think we might need. Does anyone have any questions?"

They didn't. Alex and Brent started loading the van. I took the letter and note, put them into a file folder, and headed toward the stairs. Watch out, Simon Blankenship. Rachel Buchanan is coming.

CHAPTER SEVEN

Why Can't It Be Easy?

Things nearly blew up in our faces the next morning, thanks to Mrs. Marquardt. First of all, Mrs. Marquardt is kind of weird and disturbing. She keeps quiet and floats around the school like a ghost. You can be doing something perfectly innocent like walking down the hall and you look up and suddenly there is Mrs. Marquardt staring at you. She's a middle-aged woman, but it's impossible to tell how old she is—maybe in her forties, maybe in her sixties. Because she's always lurking around, you get the idea that maybe she doesn't like kids so much. I could see her as the villain unmasked at the end of a *Scooby-Doo* episode, saying, "I would have gotten away with it, too, if it weren't for those meddling kids!" But for some reason, Mr. Kim thinks quite highly of her and seems to respect and trust her. So we must have been missing something.

Mrs. Marquardt—an early riser like everyone at Blackthorn, the school where sleep is your enemy—was in her office when we all showed up carrying Academy duffel bags over our shoulders. As we approached from the hallway we started an animated conversation among ourselves: "Won't this camp be cool?" "We get to stay right at Quantico like real FBI agents!" "I wonder if they'll let us shoot guns?" and so on, like we were all so excited that we couldn't wait to get there.

Mrs. Marquardt gave us a stern look as we knocked and entered. She had the note on the desk in front of her. It was lying perfectly centered on her desk, and she peered over it, not touching it, like it might be poisonous or something.

"Good morning, Mrs. Marquardt. We just stopped by to say good-bye before we leave." I put an extra-cheery note in my voice. Me and Mrs. Marquardt, the best of buddies.

"Good morning, children," she said. Okay, here is a tip: If you want to get on a teenager's good side, don't ever refer to them as "children." "I was just attempting to reach Mr. Kim on his cell phone, but he is not answering. He didn't mention anything about you attending this camp. It's highly irregular."

"Wow, that's so weird. We set this up a couple of weeks ago. We've really been looking forward to it." Pilar, Alex, and Brent all nodded enthusiastically and muttered things, like "Yeah," "For sure," and "Definitely."

"Mr. Kim doesn't forget things like this. He is very responsible where the students are concerned. No one has ever left the Academy for something like this. Perhaps I should call Agent Tyler."

Uh-oh. Time for the sweat on the forehead and the clammy palms. Yeesh.

"Oh man," I said, "Mrs. Marquardt, I don't know what to tell you. We really want to go to this. It's going to be a great experience. Mr. Kim was excited that we're going."

Her eyes narrowed and she stared at the four of us.

"Really," I said. Someone please kill me now.

Mrs. Marquardt frowned down her long, pointy nose at me. Luckily, just then the phone on her desk rang.

She answered, and from her conversation we could tell it was someone in the school loading dock. Alex's job was working in the loading dock at the school. He was up to something. I looked at him, and he smiled and winked.

"I'm sure Mrs. Clausen can handle it. Oh, she's not in? Very well, I shall be there shortly."

Mrs. Marquardt hung up and returned to staring at me. Somehow I got the feeling she didn't trust me. If she only knew.

"I'm needed at the loading dock. You're going to have to wait until I return so I can call Agent Tyler and get this straightened out."

"Wow. Mrs. M." I thought maybe giving her a hip nickname like Mrs. M. might bring us closer, but she winced when I said it. Okay, so I need to work on my nicknaming skills. "The FBI van is supposed to pick us up in, like, five minutes. I'm sure once you get through to Mr. Kim, if he has any problem with it you can send someone to pick us up." We all put on our best "trust me" and "look at our cute puppy-dog eyes" faces.

Mrs. M. thought this over.

"Well, all right. I'll wait with you until the van arrives." She stood up and started to step around her desk. Oh boy. Busted. This was where it was all going to end. Then her phone rang again.

"Yes," she said. "Tell the driver . . . no, don't do that . . . no, he mustn't . . . All right, I'll be right down." She hung up. "There is an emergency in the loading dock that requires my immediate attention." She paused, clearly unhappy with the way things were going. I know I was nearly ready to pass out from the tension.

"All right. You go to your camp. I will check with Mr. Kim and verify this. If there are any irregularities, you will be recalled." She looked at us sternly. Who uses a word like "recalled" in normal conversation, I'd like to know?

We didn't waste any time saying good-bye. When we were safely out of earshot, we all gave Alex a high five.

"How did you do that?" I said.

"I made a little problem happen with the food shipment that comes in from Philly to the school each morning. I told Steve that it was all part of a practical joke and to call her at 7:30 and then again two minutes later just to make sure. But don't worry. I really did mess up the shipment. She won't realize that we've done anything. At least not until we're long gone."

"That's brilliant," Pilar said. She beamed at Alex.

"Yeah, well, always have a Plan B, I say," he said. He beamed back at Pilar. Yeah, whatever. "Unfortunately, I think Mrs. Marquardt may be the easy part of our scheme. How are we going to convince a charter jet to take off with just us four kids unsupervised?"

"Don't worry," I said. "I've got a plan."

CHAPTER EIGHT

And the Oscar Goes to Rachel Buchanan

We made it to the Charter Office at the airport by nine o'clock. Alex parked the van at the back end of the parking lot so no one in the office would see us get out by ourselves. Before we had left I had dug through the stuff I'd brought from home, and in the van I put on all my rings and earrings and teased up my hair. I wanted to look as "Beverly Hills" as possible. I put my Ray-Ban sunglasses on to complete the effect. I strode into the office having a pretend conversation on my cell phone.

"I don't know what Tad could have been thinking! Taking Mitzi to Spago's after Winter Ball in the Jaguar XL? That is *so* last year," I said to no one.

There was a middle-aged guy behind the counter. He looked up as I came in. I smiled and he smiled back, and I held up a finger as if to say I'd be with him when I finished my so-important call.

"Listen, darling, I've got to go. When I'm home on break we will turn Rodeo Drive into a smoking hole in the ground. There is simply no place to shop here. I mean, the mall? Please. Anyway, gotta run. Kiss kiss. Ciao!"

I snapped my phone shut and launched into diva mode.

"I'm Rachel Buchanan. My daddy has arranged for us to take a charter flight to our environmental conference in Hawaii. I assume you have our reservation?"

He picked up a file folder on the counter and smiled.

"Hello, Miss Buchanan. My name is Frank Hansen, owner of the company. I have all of your material right here."

"Good. Let's get going. We have dolphins to save," I said.

That was when Mr. Hansen frowned. Uh-oh.

"Don't you have an adult going with you?"

"No. Since Daddy made the reservation, and Buchanan Enterprises is paying for the flight, the school decided we could fly on our own. We're being met in Hawaii by a representative from the conference." I put a heavy emphasis on "Buchanan Enterprises" because I had a feeling I was going to need the full weight of Charles Buchanan pretty soon.

"I'm afraid there's been a mistake. We can't fly unaccompanied minors."

Like now.

"Are you serious? I can't believe this. My father—Charles Buchanan, I'm sure you've heard of him—is going to be *so* furious. Why weren't we told this? Now we're going to miss the

conference and dolphins will die and it will all be your fault!"
Mr. Hansen gulped and started looking through the papers in
the file.

"I'm very sorry, Ms. Buchanan . . . but our policy clearly
states . . ."

I held up my hand and reached into my pocket for the cell
phone. I pretended to dial my dad.

"Hello, Theresa, it's Rachel." I put a near-hysterical sob in
my voice. "Is my daddy there?"

Mr. Hansen looked a little nervous. He knew who my father
was and he could see maybe this wasn't going to work out so
well for him. At the very least, he'd be out a huge fee for the
flight. I launched into a full-fledged wail.

"We're at the airport and this mean man is giving us problems. Apparently he doesn't want to take us because of some
policy about unescorted minors. Daddy *knows* how important
the dolphins are to me. I want him to fix it!"

I covered the phone with my hand like I didn't want
"Theresa" to hear me and addressed Mr. Hansen again.

"I don't know what kind of operation you are running here,
mister, but my father will have plenty to say to you. You could
have gotten a lot of business from Buchanan Enterprises out of
this, because my daddy loves me and wants me happy. And now
the dolphins are going to die!" I started to cry. Pilar, Brent, and
Alex just stared at me openmouthed.

I took my hand away from the phone and spoke into it
again.

"I don't care if he's meeting with the governor, Theresa!

There is a really mean man here and he's not going to fly us and I want Daddy to fix it! Didn't I tell you there are dolphin lives depending on this? Not to mention the poor humpback whales? I want you to make sure that Daddy never uses this company again, and I want him to get Marvin to file a lawsuit because I can't get to the conference and the whales and dolphins . . ."

"Miss Buchanan!" Mr. Hansen shouted at me and waved his arms. "Miss Buchanan, please, it's okay. You're all seventeen years of age, aren't you?" he asked.

Everyone nodded. "Well, of course we're seventeen," I said.

"Great, then, we can fly seventeen-year-olds. Unaccompanied seventeen-year-olds are okay." He stopped and rubbed his forehead for a minute. I felt bad jerking the guy around, but we had a supervillain to thwart and we were in a hurry. I starting chanting in my head: *Don't ask for ID, don't ask for ID, don't ask for ID or we're screwed.*

"Are you sure? Because I can talk to my father. The governor won't mind waiting." I said.

"No need, no need, we'll get you to Hawaii. All the paperwork is in order and the flight has been paid for. Please, really, there is no reason to upset your father. We'll get you on your flight."

"Never mind, Theresa, he's taking us," I said, and flipped the phone shut.

Thirty minutes later we were airborne. The jet was small but comfortable. We sat in seats two by two, facing each other.

"That was an epic performance," said Brent, laughing. Brent, I decided, had a very nice laugh when he decided to reveal it.

"Yeah, I'm a little out of practice playing the Beverly Hills brat. I have friends who are a lot better at it than me."

"Well, it looked good and it worked," he said.

Pilar was laughing, too. "I can't believe you," she said. "You certainly have guts, I'll say that. I would never be able to bluff my way through things like you do."

I smiled at her praise. I thought to myself how funny it was that I grew up around people who acted like that on a regular basis. They were always using their parents' influence or money to get what they wanted. I guess I just never really cared that much. I wasn't interested in that whole "social strata" thing. Luckily I saw enough of that behavior to know how to use it sometimes.

It was a long flight, and we spent most of it talking and catching up on our sleep. While we talked, Brent reached over and took my watch off my wrist again. He pulled a small tool out of his bag and started fiddling with it. Probably installing a laser or something.

It turned out that Alex had a story like mine. Only, instead of coming from a rich family in Beverly Hills, he came from a poor family in a small town in South Dakota. Alex told us that when he turned thirteen he started to get into trouble. First it was fighting, and then he started shoplifting from some of the local businesses. His parents tried to crack down on him, but nothing they did worked. He got suspended from school a lot and brought home in a police car more than a few times.

Then he blew up the Fourth of July parade.

Well, more or less. His little town was the county seat, and every year they had a Fourth of July parade that wound through the small downtown. The first vehicle in the parade was one of the town fire trucks. While the parade was forming, Alex punched a small hole in the tire of the truck and the air slowly leaked out. It went totally flat when it was almost at the end of the parade route, so the entire parade, marching bands, beauty queens, and all, were at a dead stop in the middle of town. Meanwhile, Alex had climbed on top of a building nearby, and while the parade was stuck right below him and the bands were marching in place and everyone was milling around waiting for the truck to be moved, Alex set off his own fireworks display.

He had managed to "borrow" most of the town's fireworks that were supposed to be used in the fireworks display that evening. All of a sudden, rockets and streamers started exploding right over the middle of the town. People freaked and started running in different directions, and it was total chaos. Fortunately nobody got hurt, but one of the rockets landed on a building across the street and set the roof on fire. Of course, the fire department was right there and it got put out right away, but a policeman saw Alex up on the roof laughing and he was busted.

He got into a lot of trouble. People in his hometown were really upset with him for ruining the Fourth of July, and the guy who owned the building that caught on fire was going to sue Alex's folks unless they did something about their troublesome kid. His parents couldn't afford to hire a good lawyer. He was headed for Juvenile Detention. So just like me, the judge sent him to Blackthorn instead. He'd been there a little over three years.

It's funny how people turn out. Looking at Alex now, seeing how serious he was all the time, and how devoted he was to Mr. Kim, I had a hard time imagining him being a little hellion in South Dakota.

I turned to Brent and said, "So what's your story? How'd you end up here?"

Out of the corner of my eye I saw Pilar and Alex look at each other and wince.

"I don't have a story," he said.

"What? Come on, we've all got a story. What's yours?"

"I don't like to talk about it," he said.

"Oh, you're among friends. I'd just like to know—"

Brent stood up. "You don't know me, okay?"

He moved to the back of the jet and sat down, a sad expression on his face. I looked at Pilar and Alex, and they both shook their heads like they were telling me not to push it. Hmm. Another mystery. He should know better.

So while Brent sat in the back of the plane sulking and working on my watch, I was forced to sit there and listen to Pilar and Alex murmur back and forth to each other. Every so often Pilar would laugh at something Alex said or she'd punch him on the shoulder cutely. Ugh. After a while I moved a couple of rows away, because it was getting a little too sweet for me and, well, I still didn't see what she saw in the guy. Geez.

About an hour later Brent came back to the front of the cabin and took a seat next to me. He handed me my watch. It looked the same.

"Did you do something to this?" I asked.

"Yeah. Back in the situation room, I looked through some of the cabinets for stuff that might come in handy." He took the watch from me and, using the small tool, took the back off again. He pointed to a small black dot in the inside of the watch.

"This is a special microchip that emits a locator signal, which can be read on a special GPS unit that I also brought with me. If we get separated or lost, I'll be able to find you. I mean, I'll be able to find everyone. Because I'll put one in everyone's watch, of course, not just yours. So if we have to split up or something—you know, or can't find each other . . ." He was stammering and even blushing a little, for some weird reason.

"Neat!" I said. Actually it *was* neat. I was still new to all of the espionage stuff, and besides that I tend to get lost very easily. Knowing that someone could find me by pushing a button was reassuring.

"What else did you bring?"

"A few things I thought might come in handy." He took off his backpack and opened it to show me. I had no idea what most of it was, but there were all kinds of small electrical gadgets, a flashlight, microcassette recorders, and a laptop computer. I gasped for a second when I saw a gun, thinking he'd taken a weapon from one of the lockers. But it was only a flare gun, he explained. He thought it might come in handy. I felt relieved that somebody was so prepared. He collected all of our watches and started installing the locator chips.

Finally we touched down in Hawaii at the Hilo airport. We quickly got off the plane and headed into the terminal like we knew what we were doing. I didn't want the pilots nosing around or asking any questions, because they might notice that we didn't have a clue about what we were doing, or worse, someone might place a call to Charles and we'd be busted.

I hadn't heard a single word from Charles or Cynthia since I'd been sent to Blackthorn. That was no surprise. Out of sight, out of mind. But at some point someone at Buchanan Enterprises would discover what I'd done, and then Charles would hear about it, and since I'd hit him in his wallet he probably wasn't going to like it too much. Oh well. I'd worry about that later.

We stopped for a moment in the terminal to get our bearings. The Hilo airport was pretty small and quiet, with not a lot of activity. We were studying a big map of the Hilo area on the wall, trying to figure out what to do next, when a Hawaiian girl about our age came up to us. She was wearing a khaki safari shirt, with white shorts and hiking boots.

"Hello. You must be Mr. Kim's students? My name is Leikala. I was a graduate of Blackthorn Academy four years ago. You're to accompany me to a safe house until he arrives. Mr. Kim thought you might try to get here, so he assigned someone to keep watch on the airports on all the islands and to check arriving flights. I have a car waiting. Hurry, we must go. It's not safe."

A lot of information. A little too much information. Shields up. I was reminded of Mr. Kim's warning that we weren't supposed to trust anyone. Also, his lecture to me the other day in the *do jang*: Always do a threat assessment. I mean, I have natural trust issues anyway. But something told me this wasn't right.

This didn't sound like Mr. Kim. If he really wanted us, with all of his abilities and connections he could have tracked us down easy enough.

But here she was, obviously waiting for us. I heard Mr. Kim's voice in my head. *Simon has a vast network. Trust no one.* I studied Leikala. She was maybe a little older than us, but she looked our age. So her story about attending Blackthorn *could* be true. She had gorgeous coal-black, shoulder-length hair and eyes the color of obsidian. I decided that I hated her on sight. How did she know who we were? Or anything about this, really?

I had a bad feeling. Maybe we were being watched. Somehow Simon knew what we were doing. We needed to lose this chick, and fast.

"I'm sorry, you must have mistaken us for someone else," I said. "We're here from Los Angeles on a class trip." I looked at Pilar. She had been at Blackthorn the longest, and I wondered if she recognized this Leikala person with the beautiful hair and the impossibly perfect complexion. Pilar met my gaze and instantly understood. She studied Leikala intently for a few seconds. Then she gave me an almost imperceptible head shake. Pilar sensed that she was giving off bad vibes. I smelled a trap.

"You must be Rachel," Leikala said, reaching out to shake my hand. "Mr. Kim sends his hello. I understand your suspicion, but believe me, I'm here to help you."

Yeah, right. I looked at Pilar again just to make sure, and again she gave me a small shake of the head. For some reason she didn't believe this Leikala person either. Mr. Kim's words kept ringing through my head. *Simon has vast resources, dedicated followers, and we should trust no one* and blah blah blah. Then I looked at Brent and Alex and they were totally staring all moony-eyed at Leikala. Okay, she was beautiful, but sheesh, we're on a mission! Boys.

"Listen, ma'am, I don't know who you are or who this Mr. Kim person is, but we're not who you're looking for."

I started to push past her.

"Rachel, please." She grabbed my arm. I dropped my duffel bag, grabbed her thumb, and bent it backward off my arm, in a pressure hold that Mr. Kim had taught me.

"Watch it!" I snapped. See how much those perfectly straight and brilliant white teeth help you when I knock you on your fanny.

Alex stepped in between us and she let go of my arm.

Just then, I saw a shuttle bus for our hotel pull up to the curb in front of the building.

"Sorry lady. We're not who you're looking for. Come on, guys, there's our bus." I headed for the door, with the rest of the gang behind me. I heard Leikala coming after us and shouting something, but by then we were on the bus. She turned and ran across the drive to a waiting car. It looked like she was going to follow us.

The shuttle bus took us to the outskirts of Hilo and the Royal Hawaiian Hotel. It was a pretty nice resort property. What the heck—as long as I had hacked into Buchanan Enterprises' travel system for a jet, might as well go four-star on the hotel. We all kept staring at the car out the back window of the bus. For once I was a little too nervous to talk. Nobody else said anything either. Sometimes I thought if it wasn't for me, Alex, Pilar, and especially Brent could go weeks without uttering a single syllable. We were quiet right up until the bus pulled in to the hotel lot.

Everything in the lobby was made out of teak, and a couple of the bellmen walked up to us and put leis around our necks. Our rooms had already been paid for, so we didn't have any problem getting keys. We made plans to drop off our stuff and meet back in the hotel lobby in fifteen minutes.

Once we were in our room, Pilar and I discussed this Leikala person.

"What do you think she is up to?" Pilar asked.

"I don't know. You didn't recognize her, right?"

"No, but that doesn't mean anything. There are about four hundred students in the school. If she really graduated from Blackthorn four years ago, that would have been right about the time I got there, so it's possible I never ran across her. But there is something wrong about her. I get a funny feeling she isn't telling the whole truth."

"I'm learning to trust your 'funny feelings.' Besides, nobody with skin like that can be truthworthy," I said. "Did you see the way that Alex and Brent were googling at her? It was disgusting. She's not *that* pretty."

Pilar laughed.

"What's so funny?" I snapped. The long hours of travel plus being assaulted by a Miss Hawaii look-alike had left me a little cranky.

"You're jealous." She had a very self-satisfied smile on her face as she said it.

"I am *not* jealous."

"Are too."

"Am not."

"Yep."

"Nope."

"You're crazy!" I said. I picked up my little toiletries bag and stomped into the bathroom, slamming the door.

Me jealous. Hah! Not this chick. I mean, why would I be jealous? So this Leikala person was gorgeous and perfect-looking. But that didn't mean I was jealous. Rachel Buchanan doesn't do jealous.

I brushed my teeth, which were not as brilliantly white as Leikala's. I ran a wet washcloth over the less-than-perfect skin on my face. Then I brushed my hair, which was not remotely as thick and lustrous. Jealous. I'll show you jealous. Besides, did anyone notice how she was dressed? I mean, the girl obviously needed a shopping intervention. Maybe she should try wearing something from this decade. It's Hawaii. No one wears hiking boots in Hawaii.

I ran down Leikala several more times in my head and started to regain my sense of superiority. When I came back into the room, Pilar was sitting on her bed looking through the hotel directory. I apologized for being snippy and slamming the door. She just smiled. Why wasn't *she* jealous? I mean, she and Alex were a "thing" but he was totally checking Leikala out too. It must be that Mr. Kim's Zen stuff rubs off on you if you're at the school long enough.

"I think it's time for us to put our plan into action," I said.

"What plan is that again?" she said.

"The 'stumble around until we find something' plan."

"Oh, that one. Good plan."

I walked to the window of our room. We were on the front side of the hotel on the tenth floor, and you could see the parking lot from our window. Leikala's car was parked in one of the spaces facing the hotel entrance.

"What should we do about Leikala?" I asked Pilar.

"I don't know. She seems to know a lot about us, but she could have gotten that information from Blankenship. And here's a worrying thought. What if Blankenship has someone inside the school to keep an eye on Mr. Kim? Somebody we don't suspect. They could have figured out we were gone and told Blankenship."

"Do you think that's possible?" I asked, not mentioning that I'd already had the same thought. I was paranoid enough on my own. No need to drag anyone else down with me.

"I don't know. That little speech that Mr. Kim gave us about not trusting anyone has me all spooked," Pilar said.

"And unfortunately we can't check if she attended the school, because the records aren't online, so I can't hack into the Academy files to find out. The only other people that might know are Agent Tyler and Mrs. Marquardt, and if we call one of them we're dead," I said.

Pilar agreed.

"I think we need to ditch her if we can. Let's get Alex and Brent and head down to the lobby." I went to my Academy duffel bag and grabbed my roll of cash. I had brought $200 with me

when I came to Blackthorn four months ago and still had most of it. We didn't really go anywhere—unless we were sneaking off school grounds to foil an international network of evil spies, of course. But I knew it would come in handy at some point.

The lobby was shaped like a **T**. The elevators were off to your left and the hallway to your right led to ballrooms and meeting rooms and some of the hotel restaurants. By the bank of phones in the hallway there were a bunch of scratch pads and pens, which I used to write out a note. It said: *Sorry we got off on the wrong foot. Please come to room 1237 so we can figure out what to do. Thanks, Rachel Buchanan.*

I asked a bellman to deliver my note to the driver of the black sedan that was parked out front. I gave him a $10 bill and he hustled out the door. Then we all picked up phones and stayed out of sight until, a couple of minutes later, I saw Leikala come scurrying into the lobby and head straight for the elevator. She took the first available car and was gone.

"Come on!" I said.

We shot out the door and grabbed a taxi. I asked the driver if he knew where the big archaeological dig site was outside of town. He said he did and that the fare would be $20 and did we have the money? I showed him two twenties; he smiled and said "*Mahalo*" and off we went.

"Very slick, Raych," Pilar said.

"Yeah, she'll be confused when no one answers the door," Alex said.

"Or somebody that isn't me answers the door," I said. I had of course given her the wrong room number in the note.

Brent cleared his throat and nodded his head slightly toward the driver, signaling that maybe we shouldn't say too much in front of people we didn't know. That was one thing I didn't like about this whole spy/secret agent thing. Basically I'm a big blabbermouth, so everybody is always shushing me.

We were quiet the rest of the way to the dig site. Outside of Hilo the Hawaiian terrain looks basically like the middle of the jungle. The eastern side of the Big Island of Hawaii gets a lot of rain and so there is vegetation everywhere. It was like something out of a Tarzan or George of the Jungle movie. I half expected a loinclothed Brendan Fraser to swing by the taxi on a vine. Now, that would be cool.

The cabbie dropped us off at a dirt road that led back into the jungle to the dig site. We could see it through the trees about a half a mile away. There was a lot of scaffolding and trucks parked around it.

It didn't take us long to reach the site. It looked pretty much like a big hole in the ground, maybe a hundred feet across and about fifty or sixty feet deep. There was scaffolding around the edge and reaching down to the floor of the hole with a little lift elevator attached to it, like a window washer on a skyscraper. At the bottom, on each side of the hole, were what looked like small tunnels, going in opposite directions.

"It's a lava tube," Alex explained.

"A tube of what?" I asked.

"A lava tube. When a volcano erupts and the lava flows over the surface of the ground, the top layer will cool and harden but the lava will keep flowing underneath. Eventually molten lava flows out to a lower elevation and the empty hollow tube is left behind. The island is full of them. Early Hawaiians actually lived in them sometimes. I'll bet that's how this site was discovered." He looked at me and shrugged, like everyone in the world knew about lava tubes.

I was surrounded by brainiacs.

Amazingly we walked right up to the dig site and nobody asked who we were or why we were there. Of course, none of us had ever been to an archaeological dig before, so we didn't have the slightest idea what to do. There were about thirty people at work, and it wasn't like we could walk up to any of them and say, "Excuse me? Are you a Mithrian? Intent on world domination? Like to steal priceless artifacts? Step away from the hole, please." I was sure that Blankenship would have people here undercover, looking for clues about where the artifact was hidden. He would want people on the inside so that if anything valuable was found he could move to steal it right away. We would have to be careful about what we said and whom we talked to. The only trouble was, we were eventually going to have to talk to *someone*.

So we stood around, waiting to stumble over a clue. Finally a guy in shorts and a T-shirt and hiking boots came up.

"Can I help you with something?" he asked.

"Yes, we're from the Institute. We're to meet our professor, Dr. Kim, here at the site today," I said.

"The Pfizer Institute?" he asked. Doh! Of course, there would have to be a real institute. Dang the luck.

"Uh, no, we're actually from the Buchanan Institute. We're

in the Antiquities and Medieval History Department there. Dr. Kim arranged for us to intern on the dig, and we were supposed to start today." It sure sounded good, right? I almost said the Blackthorn Institute, but I didn't want to give anything away.

"I'm Dr. Reynolds. I'm in charge of the site here. How come I don't know anything about this? I've never heard of the Buchanan Institute."

Sweat was forming on my forehead—and not from the humidity.

"Really? It's the Buchanan Institute in eastern Pennsylvania, near Philadelphia. There must be some mix-up in the paperwork. Hasn't Dr. Kim arrived yet?"

"I've never heard of Dr. Kim either . . . "

Suddenly, like a bad penny, Leikala was there. She must have arrived without us noticing. She barged into the middle of our group and grabbed Dr. Reynolds's hand and started pumping it vigorously.

"I'm sorry for the confusion, Dr. Reynolds. I was supposed to be the university liaison with Dr. Kim's students, and I just learned a short while ago that you had not been informed."

"Hello, Leikala." Dr. Reynolds frowned. "What is going on here?"

"It's part of the university student-exchange program. These students are here to participate in the dig as part of their curriculum."

"I don't know anything about that," he said. He was starting to sound really annoyed.

"I know, and I apologize for the mix-up. However, since

they are here now, perhaps we can just put them to work?" She kind of fluttered her eyelashes at the professor when she said it. Made me want to punch them both.

"Leikala, what about their permits? You know the state regulations are very strict here. If they don't have permits, they are not allowed on the site."

"I guess you're right," Leikala said. "Tell you what. Why don't I leave Alex, Pilar, and Brent with you and I'll take this young lady into Hilo to the university office. They must have the paperwork there. Maybe you can have someone show them around while we're gone?"

Dr. Reynolds frowned, then nodded. "I guess that would be all right. As long as you get back right away with the paperwork." Leikala smiled and assured him that would be the case. Then she turned to me and said, "Shall we go?"

We were stuck. If I didn't go with her, our cover was blown and we'd be in more trouble than any of us could imagine. But I didn't trust this Leikala any farther than the end of her perfectly pert little nose. Still, we didn't seem to have a choice.

"Sure," I said. "We'll get this all straightened out and be right back. But tell you what—Pilar should come with us. She's so much better at that paperwork stuff than me." Then I started to laugh. I laugh when I'm nervous and scared. Don't know why, but there you go. Pilar elbowed me in the ribs sharply. The pain made me stop laughing. I watched Leikala for a reaction, but her perfectly chiseled face didn't betray anything. I hated her even more. She just smiled and nodded.

I looked at Alex and Brent. "And while we're gone, you guys

make yourselves useful. Don't stand around like you're in a museum or something. Remember what Dr. Kim is looking for." Alex nodded. He got it. If we don't come back, do what you can to find the artifact. That was most important.

Leikala's car was parked not too far away. When she reached it, she opened the back door and held it like a chauffeur.

Before I got in, I looked back at Alex and Brent. Alex gave a little wave and said, "Hey, if for some reason you don't get back in time, we'll meet you at the hotel! Better not be late for dinner or there will be fireworks." He smiled like everything was normal. What the heck did that mean? Fireworks? Is that some kind of code word?

I slid into the backseat next to Pilar. Leikala looked over her shoulder and smiled as she started the car.

"Well, you guys led me on a merry chase today. Well done," she said.

"How did you know where to find us?" I asked. No sense in pretending we weren't who we were anymore. She had us.

"It was the logical first choice since you know about the artifact, you'd start at the dig site."

"What artifact?" I said, playing dumb. Leikala smirked at me like it was time for me to drop my facade, but I stared her down.

"Did you really talk to Mr. Kim?" I said after an awkward pause. I glanced over at Pilar, but she was intently studying the back of Leikala's head. Maybe, just maybe, Leikala was telling the truth and everything would be okay.

Except it wasn't.

Because when Leikala pulled out on the main road, she turned in the opposite direction of Hilo, and as she did, the back doors of the car locked shut and a dark black glass partition slid out of the front seat up to the ceiling of the car, sealing us off from the driver.

We were trapped.

CHAPTER NINE

We Meet Again

We tried the doors. They were locked tight. We pounded on the windows, but they were tinted and I doubted that anyone could see in. Not that there was any traffic going by anyway.

I pulled my phone out of my pocket and turned it on. But it gave me a "Signal Not Available" sign on the LED screen. Stupid phone. Pilar's said the same thing. Leikala's voice came over the speakers.

"Your phones won't work. The backseat of the car is lined with a special compound that blocks the signals."

"Where are you taking us?" I said, trying to keep the fear out of my voice.

"Just enjoy the ride. By the way, I can hear you and see you. So don't try anything stupid."

I was scared. Was there anything I could do? I had a cell phone that didn't work, a wad of cash in my jeans pocket, and my Swiss Army knife. Maybe I could hack my way through the side of the car to freedom. Ha. Pilar didn't have anything in the way of weapons. Our hearts were beating a thousand beats a minute, but we were out of ideas.

We drove for quite a while, turning frequently. We seemed to be headed into the interior of the island. The terrain became more mountainous and covered with even thicker vegetation. We sat there staring out the tinted windows and watching the countryside go by.

After a while, the car slowed and we pulled off the road onto a path that led into the rain forest. The trees and bushes were very close to the car. Then the car seemed to drive into the side of a mountain, and as we pulled in, I could see that we were now inside a huge compound built into the mountain. Great. It was another secret hideout just like the one at Blackthorn. Doesn't anybody use plain old barns or garages anymore? Why not old, abandoned warehouses somewhere, like normal crooks?

The car stopped and I could hear the locks on the back doors release. A big, burly guy in a black jumpsuit opened the door on my side. He looked like he'd had a healthy dose of steroids with his Cheerios that morning. He grabbed my arm and pulled me out of the car. Another guy that could have been his twin was hustling Pilar out the other side.

We were in a large room with about six cars and trucks parked in it. There were a handful of people milling around and watching us. They were all wearing the same black skintight jumpsuits. Leikala got out of the car and turned to face me. The behemoth holding my arm let go for a second. That was when I launched the best spin kick of my life right at Leikala's head. It was a beauty.

Unfortunately she was ready for it and blocked it easily. This told me she had some martial arts training—probably more than me. Maybe she wasn't lying about going to Blackthorn after all. I was about to go for her eyes when King Kong grabbed me from behind. Lucky for her.

"Enough," she yelled. "You are so predictable. I don't know why Simon is so fascinated by you."

So there was the proof. As if we hadn't guessed already, she was working for Blankenship. And this must be some kind of Mithrian hideout. Great. Just great. Could I be any more lame? I mean, I get us all the way out of the school and on a plane to Hawaii, and I'm not there five minutes before the bad guy captures me. Maybe this whole secret-agent "fighting the forces of darkness" thing was not a good career choice for me. Perhaps I should consider switching to the food services industry or maybe being a bowling alley attendant.

"Let me go!" I tried to kick backward and get Kong in the shins, but it was like kicking a steel pipe. He just laughed.

"Take them to the holding cells. Simon will be here shortly." She turned and started across the room.

"Hey! Leikala!" I yelled. She stopped.

"Yes?"

"You have a big zit on your lip!"

Her hand started to fly to her face before she stopped and scowled at me.

"Take her now!" she yelled.

Ha! Score one for Rachel Buchanan. If you can't kick a bad girl in the head, go after her complexion. Childish, I know. But I needed to land a couple of shots to help rebuild my fast-crumbling self-esteem.

Kong and his twin took us down a hallway. I tried to look around the facility to see if I could learn anything. A bunch of old crates and stuff were stacked around that said "U.S. Navy," so maybe this was an old military installation left over from the war. I had read a little about the Big Island on the flight over, and there was a section in the guidebook that said the U.S. military used it for training during World War II. This was probably some old bomb shelter or something that the Mithrians had expanded.

Finally I was unceremoniously shoved into an empty room. There were a couple of thin mattresses on the floor and nothing else. I heard the door being locked behind me, and realized they must have taken Pilar to another room. I was alone.

I tried to organize my thoughts. I had to assume the room was bugged and they could watch me. I still had my cell phone that didn't work. I still had my Swiss Army knife too, but I didn't think I could take on a whole compound of Mithrians with that.

Basically I was stuck. I paced some more and then sat on the mattress. There wasn't much to do except wait for Simon to show up. Which of course he eventually did.

He came into the room without even knocking. I have to say this is one rude person. Lies, steals, tries to take over the world, and then walks in on you without knocking. He was wearing a black jumpsuit like everyone else, plus the same gold medallion with the engraving of a bull's head on it that he'd worn on the ship.

Leikala and the steroid twins entered the room behind him. She had changed into the same jumpsuit everyone else was wearing. I stood up.

"Ms. Buchanan," he said. "So lovely to see you again."

"Charmed," I said. Not.

He laughed.

"You are a prickly one, aren't you? But you are also the living reincarnation of a goddess, and I suppose that requires a certain amount of bravado."

Mr. Kim was right. Simon was bonkers, and for some reason he thought I was this Etherea person reborn. But to hear him say it made it real somehow. I guess a small part of me had hoped maybe Mr. Kim was wrong—that Blankenship really didn't have this whole "Rachel is a living goddess" thing going on. Part of me had wanted to believe that he was just really, really angry with me for messing up his ship and stealing his book. And then perhaps after we'd discussed our feelings, we'd shake hands, apologize for the misunderstanding, and go our separate ways.

But nope. Here he was standing right in front of me, confirming Mr. Kim's theory. Whoo boy. Right. Me a goddess? A goddess of shopping, perhaps. A goddess of getting out of doing homework, definitely. But not Etherea, the goddess of light. I guess Mr. Kim knew Blankenship pretty well.

"Whatever," I said. "That whole 'living goddess' thing? I don't even have my driver's license yet, and I'm pretty sure if I were a goddess I'd at least be able to drive. So I'd say this has all been a big misunderstanding. Now you can just let me and my friend go and we'll forget the whole thing."

"Don't try to deny your destiny, Ms. Buchanan. Or, I should say, Etherea. I'm quite convinced, and so is Jonathon. He told me himself that he believes it is true. Etherea has been reborn, just as prophesied, and it is you."

Mr. Kim had told him that? What? When did that happen? Very smart, Mr. Kim.

"You know Mr. Kim is on his way to rescue us, don't you?" I said.

Leikala had moved to a position near Simon, and when I said that they looked at each other. Just a quick glance. Weird.

"I wouldn't worry about your Mr. Kim coming to save you. From what I saw of you in Washington, I imagine he doesn't even know you're here, does he?"

I tried to keep my face from showing anything. But it was no use. For a moment I couldn't think of anything to say.

"I thought so," said Simon. "Your timing is impeccable, Ms. Buchanan," he went on. "Tonight we are planning a ceremony in your honor. Then we will find the artifact and leave the island. Jonathon will never find us."

A little ray of hope entered my mind. If there was going to be a ceremony somewhere else than here, maybe there would be a chance to get away in transit. Plus, that meant he hadn't found the artifact yet. Aha.

"What type of ceremony? Luau? Dance party? Will there be a DJ or a live band?" I asked.

Blankenship was getting good at ignoring me.

"I'm sure Jonathon has told you that it was Etherea who banished Mithras to the underworld. Tonight we take the first step to release him from his unwanted exile."

"How? You don't even have all the artifacts yet. And you can't bring this bull guy to life without them. So isn't your ceremony a little premature?"

"Certainly there is more work to be done. But we must go in stages, and your arrival here has brought us an unexpected gift. Something we mean to take advantage of. Although I may dispose of you anyway, just to see what happens to the prophecy then."

Gulp. Okay. Not so good. "Dispose" of me. But something was going on here. I mean, Simon had been planning this for years, so I think he threatened to kill me just to spook me. If he really did things out of order, it might screw up years of scheming on his part. I didn't think he'd take that chance. But he *was* crazy. Then I started worrying that he'd deciphered the map and found the artifacts. Maybe if he found the one here on the island he could summon Mithras. Then I was toast.

Time to be distracting.

"Have you found any of the other relics?" I asked. I doubted he would give anything away, but then, the guy was a huge egomaniac. If he did have all the artifacts, surely he wouldn't be able to resist rubbing it my face.

"As I'm sure your Mr. Kim has told you, I have tremendous resources at my disposal—thousands of followers who are dedicated to the cause of summoning Mithras. Finding the relics has been easy, really." I was sure he was lying. He didn't have them. He was bluffing and trying to draw me out to see if I knew anything.

"Sure. I guess when you threaten, maim, intimidate, and kill people, it's a real motivator," I said.

Blankenship laughed. The guy has the most evil laugh you'll ever hear.

"Indeed. Killing those who disappoint you is an effective management method. I highly recommend it. But you'll get a firsthand look at some of my methods this evening. And then I suggest you think about the possible benefits of working *with* me." He smirked at me and turned to leave. I wanted to keep him talking. Perhaps I could trick him into giving up more information.

"Let me get this straight, bull boy," I said. "First you want to destroy Etherea, who is supposedly me, and then you want me to join you? First of all: Ick. No, thanks. I mean, look at your uniforms. That ninja look jumped the shark two seasons ago."

Leikala flashed me an evil look. Mithras glanced at her and she shrugged her shoulders. It was clear they didn't know what "jumped the shark" meant. Losers.

"You know, went out of fashion. Lost all hope of any hipness. Became irrelevant." I used my most superior tone. Leikala just kept glaring at me.

I pointed to my lip and said, "Don't worry, a little Clearasil will clear that right up."

She started toward me, but Blankenship put out his arm and stopped her.

"I hate to be melodramatic, Ms. Buchanan, but I think you will find joining me to be much better than the alternative."

"And what is that?" I asked. I suspected I already knew the answer.

"Why, death, of course."

And with that he turned and left the room.

CHAPTER TEN

Out of the Darkness

The waiting was agony. First of all, about an hour after Mithras left I really had to use the bathroom. As the need to go reached crisis stage, I had to pound on the door for fifteen minutes before Dumb opened it. He led me to a bathroom down the hall. That was a relief. When he brought me back, he shoved me roughly into the room again.

"I'll bet high school was the best seven years of your life," I said to him. His eyes narrowed like he didn't get it.

"You see, most people only go to high school for four years. That's why it's funny when I say high school was the best seven—" He slammed the door in my face before I could finish.

A short while after that, Dumber came into the room with a tray of fruit and bread and some guava juice in a pitcher.

He set it on the floor and left.

We'd been able to sleep and eat on the plane ride over, but my body clock was all messed up. I was running on pure adrenaline. When I saw the tray of food I realized how hungry I was, and since I didn't think Mithras would try to poison me before he killed me in his stupid ceremony that night, I dug right in.

After more waiting I heard the door being unlocked, and Leikala and Dumb and Dumber came into the room. No Blankenship.

"What? Where's Simon? Too busy polishing his bull's horns?" Leikala stepped toward me and launched a round kick. I didn't move or flinch. I figured (make that hoped) that Simon wouldn't want us roughed up before his big ceremony. Luckily, I was right. Leikala's kick stopped about an inch from my temple. She was good. I had to give her that.

"You know I could kill you so easily," she said.

"Maybe. But I don't think your boss would be real happy about that. That's the trouble with being a hench-girl. If you were in charge, you could just kill me and get it over with. But when you're second fiddle, there's always someone you have to answer to."

"Hah! Like you don't jump each time your precious Mr. Kim snaps his fingers."

"Sure. We all pretty much do what Mr. Kim tells us to. But the big difference, Leikala, is that if we want, we walk away and do our own thing. Once you've thrown in with Mithras, I don't think he lets you leave. So an almost-smart girl like you will never end up running things. How sad."

The whole time we were having this conversation, Leikala kept her foot cocked an inch from my face. I think she was trying to demonstrate how long she could hold her fighting stance. What a show-off. Now she brought her foot down.

"You're going to know a lot about *sad* very soon," she said.

She nodded at Dumb and Dumber. I noticed then that Dumber was carrying a little folding screen. As he took it to a corner of the room and set it up, Dumb hung a long white gown on a hanger from the top of the screen. Then they left.

"No separate dressing room?" I said. "You Mithrians must have to operate on a budget. Pretty funny when your boss is supposed to be one of the wealthiest guys in the world. I mean, couldn't he buy some furniture, for crying out loud?"

"Shut up and change," Leikala said.

I walked behind the screen and took a look at the robe. It looked familiar somehow.

"Are you sure you don't have anything else?" I called over the screen. "I'm not really a *robe* type of girl. Is there an Old Navy store nearby? They're having a huge sale this week on performance fleeces. We could save money and be stylish all at the same time."

"Shut up and change."

I really didn't have much of an option. I didn't think I could take Leikala. Plus the steroid twins were right outside the door and they'd be on me in a second. Too bad I didn't have a secret gas pellet or a stun gun or even a table leg. If I survived this I was going to talk to Mr. Kim about getting a lot more spy gear.

I decided to just drop the robe over my clothes. It was all

white and made of some kind of flimsy material that felt like thick gauze. Almost like it was made out of soft metal or really light chain mail, if that makes sense.

Once I had it on, I stepped from behind the screen.

"What is this I'm wearing?" I asked.

"It is a re-creation of Etherea's Gown of Light. You will be wearing it in the ceremony." Aha. I had seen something like this in the painting of Mithras and Etherea that Mr. Kim had shown me.

"Hmm. Well, here's hoping you Mithrians fail in that 'world conquest' thing, if this is how everyone will have to dress. You clearly have no fashion sense."

"You won't be around to see it anyway," she said, smiling evilly.

"So where is this ceremony happening? Someplace nice, I hope."

"Wouldn't you like to know," she said.

"Well, duh. Of course I want to know. That's why I'm pumping you for information. Don't you know when you're being tricked into revealing secrets? Geez, what kind of dense supervillains are you people? No wonder you were dumb enough to sign on with Blankenship."

"Simon is a great man! He has a vision. Those of us who are loyal to him will have enormous power when Mithras is summoned forth." She had a dreamy look on her face like she had a crush on the guy or something. Yuck. Major yuck.

"But if you really went to Blackthorn, then you know Mr. Kim, and—"

"I never went to your stupid school, you idiot. That was a lie."

She spun around and left without another word.

More time passed. By now I had been inside the compound for about six hours, according to my watch. Surely Alex and Brent had gone to the police by now. They would be looking for us, but they wouldn't know where. And we were hidden inside a mountain. They could fly right over us and not see us. So we were going to have to do something on our own.

The only trouble with that plan was that I wasn't very good at escaping. I was good at getting caught. I was, in fact, excellent at getting caught. If there were an Olympics for getting caught by bad guys, I'd win the gold medal. Not to mention my "walking right into a trap" skills. *Okay, Rachel. Calm down. Think.*

Pilar had to be somewhere nearby. So if I could get out of this and find her, maybe at least one of us could get out of here and get help. Break it down to steps. First step: Get out of this room.

I tried the door again just in case. Still locked. So I was going to have to get someone to open it. My eyes fell on the light switch. Mr. Kim had taught us a lot about turning circumstances to our advantage. So what could I turn to my advantage? Darkness and surprise.

I went to the door and started pounding on it. "Hey!" I yelled. "I need to use the bathroom again. Hurry up!" I kept it up for several minutes. Finally I heard the key scratch its way into the lock. Someone was coming. Quickly I switched off the light and stood to the side of the doorway. It was too dark to tell whether it was Dumb or Dumber who opened the door and started into the room.

"What the—" I heard him say when he saw the light was out, but that was all he said, because right then I kicked him as hard as I could in the side of his knee. He yelped and staggered to the side but didn't go down. It was like kicking a piece of concrete, but at least I had hurt him a little bit. And I was about to hurt him more.

One of the first rules Mr. Kim had taught me about self-defense was the importance of the human head in a fight. Mr. Kim's credo was "where the head goes, the body soon follows." So when Dumb or Dumber yelled and staggered toward me, I grabbed two handfuls of his hair and yanked him straight over onto the floor. He screeched in pain (because I was really yanking hard—teach him to lock me in some dumb old room) and his head hit the concrete floor with a thump. He lay still. He was really going to be ticked at me when he woke up. But for the moment he was out cold.

I checked his pockets and found a set of keys. I stepped over him into the hallway, pulled the door closed, and locked him inside. There was no one around. If the room had been under surveillance I was hoping he'd been the one watching me, so I had a few minutes before anyone noticed he was gone.

I went to the door straight across from the room I'd been in and found the right key for the lock. Empty. I found Pilar in the third door I tried. She sprang to her feet.

"Rachel, are you okay?" she said.

"No time to talk," I said. "We need to get out of here."

We went back out into the hallway, just in time to hear the doorjamb of my cell crack with a loud snap as Dumb shoved his way through it. He came staggering out of the room limping and holding his head, but he saw us and started to yell.

Before he could get a sound out, Pilar vaulted across the hallway and planted a round kick right in his stomach. It knocked him back into the wall, but the guy was like a piece of iron. With a grunt of rage he pushed himself off the wall and swung wildly at Pilar.

Nimbly she stepped inside the punch and captured his arm with her hands. Then, almost faster than I could see, she moved out under his arm and twisted it behind him. Dumb groaned and tried to wrench his arm away, but he couldn't get the right angle. Then Pilar launched a kick to Dumb's groin and he went down with all the fight gone out of him. He didn't move. Apparently he'd passed out.

"Wow. Remind me never to borrow your hairbrush without asking first," I said. Pilar just shrugged, like this was something she did every day. I had to hand it to Mr. Kim. It seemed the martial arts were very useful in this type of work.

We stood in the hallway trying to decide what to do. One direction led back to the main compound. A few yards in the other direction, the lights on the ceiling ended and we couldn't see beyond that point. But we knew where the other direction led—straight to Mithras and his cronies. Neither of us wanted to charge blindly into the darkness, but we had no choice. We started to run.

CHAPTER ELEVEN

Into the Light

Soon we were in total darkness. The finished hallway ended and now we were running down a lava tube or a tunnel. It was too dark to tell which, but since we were on the Big Island, which is basically a giant volcano, I decided to assume lava tube. Luckily the surface of a lava tube is mostly smooth, so we didn't have to worry about stumbling around too much. We did slow down a bit, though, because frankly, if the tube were to end suddenly, I didn't feel like doing a Wile E. Coyote into solid rock. Personally I'd rather have the giant anvil dropped on my head.

"Hope this isn't a dead end," I said. "That would definitely make this a below-average escape attempt."

"I doubt it," Pilar said. "Most of these tubes surface eventually. We just need to keep going."

"How do you know that?" I said. "What if it stops?"

"I don't think it will. We studied lava tubes in Physical Science last year. And besides, do you feel that breeze on your face? Fresh air has to be coming in from somewhere."

Of course, I didn't know any of this because . . . well, duh, how often in life are you going to need detailed knowledge of lava tubes? But ever since I got to Blackthorn I'd been feeling like Pilar, Alex, and Brent were a lot smarter than me. Of course, they worked hard, and did stuff like study and pay attention in class, whereas my study habits were somewhat . . . let's say, fluid. But right then I made myself a vow that if I was going to jaunt all over the globe fighting evil megalomaniacs I was going to have to start concentrating more on my academics. You never know when you might pick up something you need.

Still, it was a little depressing to be outsmarted by the three of them all the time. Time to engage in some basic pulling of the chain.

"Well, I hope it's not just cave wind," I said.

"Cave wind?"

"Yeah, you know, cave wind. It's caused by a thermodynamic inversion of air pressure when the subsurface rock formations in a cave change temperature as the cave elevation rises or lowers. The inversion causes self-generating wind in caves as the warm and cold air moves around. I just hope we're not feeling cave wind and thinking it's fresh air," I said. I had no idea what I'd just said, and as far as I knew there was no such thing as "cave wind," but it sounded cool, didn't it?

"I've never heard of cave wind," she said. If I could have

96

seen her face in the darkness, I'm sure it would have been all scrunched up as she tried to figure out why she didn't know about cave wind. Man, I'm good.

"Yeah, well, it's in all the best caves. Let's keep moving," I said. I needed to change the subject, because I had exhausted my "knowledge" of cave wind.

We kept a slow trot going for quite a while and then I started to notice that the darkness was getting lighter. We had to be getting closer to the surface. Then, sure enough, we came to a bunch of bushes and vines, and when we pushed through we found ourselves in the open air.

Except, somehow, we'd taken a wrong turn and ended up on the moon.

Of course, it wasn't really the moon, but it looked like it. Later I would learn that we had come out in an old lava field in Volcanoes National Park, which is on the southern end of the Big Island. Except for the vegetation that clung to the side of the mountain, it was pretty bare—mostly just rocks and dirt. It was a huge, kind of scary-looking place. Here and there you could see jets of steam hissing up from the ground. Nothing like big puffs of steam coming up out of the earth to remind you that you are standing on top of a giant lake of molten fire.

But we didn't have time to contemplate it. We had to get out of here. We both pulled out our cell phones, but there was still no signal. Maybe that compound that Leikala mentioned had messed them up permanently somehow. Dang.

Blankenship and Leikala and the others were probably right behind us. We took a quick glance around. There was no one anywhere that we could see. Although it was still light out, it was getting dark and the park was probably closed. We looked out across the field and saw that about a mile away it started to slope up another mountain. There looked to be a trail there that led back into the jungle, and we could see a small wooden structure, maybe a hut or a ranger station or something. We took off across the floor of the valley as quickly as we could, jumping over and around lava boulders and the rocks that lined the valley floor. It was slow going, and we had to be careful because the surface was rough and uneven. If one of us fell or twisted an ankle, we'd never get away.

I kept looking over my shoulder to where we'd come out, expecting that madman Blankenship and his band of merry geeks to pop out at any moment. But so far there was no sign of them. Finally, after what seemed like a long time, we made it across the moonscape to the trail. We sprinted up and saw that what we had thought was a hut or a cabin wasn't that at all. It was just a little observation station with a roof on it and a map along one wall that showed the whole park. There was no phone or anything. How could they not have a phone here? I mean, they have phones everywhere now—hello!

While I was grousing about our lack of telecommunications, Pilar was studying the map. She quickly figured out where we were and what route we needed to take to get out of here. She turned and looked south to where the valley ended. You could see the lava flow where it breached the surface and flowed into the ocean, rising up in a huge cloud of steam. Pilar let out a yelp.

"Did you just yelp?" I said.

"That's it! That's got to be it," she said.

"What's got to be it?" I said.

"Right here. Pele's Point." She pointed to a section of the map that jutted out into the ocean. Then she pointed to the lava flow again. "In the *Book of Seraphim* Flavius wrote all of these riddles that were supposed to be clues to where the artifacts were hidden. The riddle I'm thinking of says:

"*Mithras walks with Hades' handmaiden,*
As she strolls seaward from her garden paradise.
There lies hidden the golden vessel that shall
Bring our King to life.

"That's got to be it. I didn't make the connection until just now. Hades was the Roman god of the Underworld. Pele is the Hawaiian goddess of the fiery underground where volcanoes come from. That must be where the artifact is hidden! At this point on the island the lava flows right into the sea. Pele 'strolling seaward'—that has to be it."

I had no idea what she was talking about, but she was all excited and jumping up and down.

Just then I heard a noise coming from across the valley floor. I looked back just in time to see Leikala, Dumber, and a slightly limping Dumb emerge from the lava tube. Uh-oh.

"We have to go back," Pilar said. "I know the artifact is here somewhere!"

"Not a good idea," I said and pointed across the valley floor to where Leikala and the Stupid twins were picking their way toward us.

"We have to search that area first! We can't let them get lucky and stumble across it." She started out of the hut toward the trail, but I ran after her and grabbed her.

"Pilar, we can't go back. They'll catch us. Try to get back to the hotel somehow and hook up with Alex and Brent. The three of you figure out a way to find that statue—fast."

"What are you going to do?" she asked.

I took a deep breath.

"I'm going to play a little game of hide-and-seek," I said.

"Rachel, they'll catch you. Simon might do something really bad this time. I can't let you do this!" She was getting very worked up.

"Pilar, there's no time for this. We don't have many options. One of us needs to get away, and we need to find that statue. You're the logical choice. You've studied the book, you know what to do. I can't even find my socks in the morning," I said.

"Stop making jokes! I won't let you do this!" She was crying now.

"We don't have a choice. You have a job to do. You need to focus on that. Now go!" I started toward the trail.

"Before you go, there's something I need to tell you," she said.

"What's that?"

"There's no such thing as cave wind." She smiled through her tears.

I smiled back and gave Pilar a quick hug.

Then I turned and ran down the path, back toward the valley we'd just crossed, taking the next steps closer to my destiny.

CHAPTER TWELVE

Run, Rachel, Run

I led them on a merry chase, zigzagging back and forth across the floor of the valley. I figured it was likely they were going to catch me, so I wanted to buy as much time as I could for Pilar to get away. I kept angling away from where we came into the valley, figuring that if they did catch me, I could use up extra time making them take me all the way back to the lava tube. I might have been able to keep it up for a lot longer, but I ran out of real estate.

At the extreme end of the park, the lava comes right out of the ground and flows down to the ocean, where it hardens in a big whoosh of steam. I had run myself into a dead end. Mithrians behind me and hot molten lava in every other direction. So they caught me. As I said, I'm excellent at getting caught.

Unfortunately, by then I was so out of breath I couldn't even think up a snappy wisecrack to keep them off guard. When they caught up with me I was bent over, hands on my knees, gasping for breath. Dumb and Dumber grabbed my arms and started dragging me back to the lava tube.

"Hey, how's that knee feeling?" I said to Dumb.

His eyes darkened and he responded by squeezing my arm very tightly. I hollered for him to stop, and Leikala hissed at him. He loosened his grip.

"That's right," I said, "you wouldn't want to damage your boss's precious cargo."

"Shut your mouth," Leikala said. "I'm sick of your talking."

I decided not to press my luck. They might push me off a cliff or something and tell Blankenship I had "accidentally" fallen to my death. We wouldn't want that.

It was dark now, and Leikala lighted our way with a flashlight. A little over an hour later, I was unceremoniously shoved back into a room just like the one I'd been in before.

I sat cross-legged on the ground and waited. At least my escape hadn't been a total washout. Hopefully Pilar had gotten away. I was really hoping she'd managed to find her way back to Hilo, but I couldn't count on it. I had no idea how far it was to the hotel from here. So I couldn't rely on them to help me, at least not yet. Keeping that relic away from Mithras was the first priority, and Pilar would understand that. I hoped.

After a long while, Dumb and Dumber and Leikala came into the room, and I stood up.

"It's time," she said.

Just for fun I feinted a kick at Dumb's sore knee. He yowled and skipped away. That cracked me up. This big doofus scared of little old me.

"Knock it off," Leikala snapped.

They took me out of the room and back into the main compound. I didn't see Simon anywhere, but there were a lot of cars and vans and he was probably in one of them.

"Where are we going?" I asked.

"Wouldn't you like to know," Leikala said.

"I thought we covered this already. Of course I'd like to know, that's why I asked. Can't you people please get some better comebacks? Do they not teach you these things in Supervillain School?"

"Just shut up," she said, and roughly shoved me toward the back of a van. Before I got in they took my cell phone and my Swiss Army knife and my wad of cash and put it in a duffel bag they stuck on the floor of the van. If I got a chance to get away, I was going to be cut off from communication, unarmed, and broke.

Dumb and Dumber got into the front seat of the van and Leikala sat in the backseat with me. All of the cars pulled out of the hidden compound and we started off in a big motorcade. They were silent on the way—big surprise.

"Anybody want to play license-plate alphabet while we drive?" I said.

"Shut up," Leikala snapped at me.

"Oh, right. In order to play, you have to actually know the alphabet, so that gives me an unfair advantage. How about we sing instead? Show tunes? 'Wheels on the Bus' anyone? 'Ninety-nine Bottles of Beer on the Wall'?" I figured if I kept it up long enough maybe I could annoy them into pushing me out of the car. We weren't going that fast. Besides, my constant chatter really got under Leikala's skin, and if she was rattled that might give me some advantage.

"Keep it up and we'll see if you can still flap your lips after I crush your larynx," Leikala said.

Okay. That didn't sound fun. But I didn't really think she'd lay a finger on me as long as her boss wanted the pleasure of killing me himself.

"Are we there yet?" I asked. No one answered me.

"How much longer?" I asked. Still no response.

Obviously they didn't know who they were dealing with, because I could keep this up as long as I needed to.

But it wasn't long before we were pulling back into the dig site. Somehow I'd had a feeling this was where we were headed.

Except for my captors, the dig site was deserted. It looked different and kind of spooky at night. Down in the center of the pit, a bonfire had been built. I didn't think it was such a good idea to start a fire on a valuable archaeological site, but I kept that thought to myself.

They herded me toward the scaffolding elevator, and we all rode it down to the bottom. Then they took me over by the bonfire and we waited.

Blankenship came strolling out of a nearby lava tube. He was wearing a robe like mine, only black. His gold medallion shone in the firelight. He also wore some type of mask or helmet with a giant pair of horns coming out of the side of it. Frankly, he looked ridiculous, like a really bad mascot for a college football team, or like some kind of twisted opera singer. He had two other Mithrians with him. There were about ten Mithrians now at the bottom of the pit, and I wasn't sure how many up at the top, if any. It was dark and I couldn't get an accurate count.

Simon started to speak.

"Children of Mithras! We stand tonight on a sacred place. Here, many hundreds of years ago, the first of our kind brought the word of Mithras to this place. We do not know what happened to them. But we know they left one of the sacred relics here for us to find. Tonight we will command a sacrifice and start on the path for Mithras' darkness to flow across the land. Begin."

I figured this was my cue. I was about to be boiled in oil, or drawn and quartered, or maybe shot out of a cannon. That would at least be a cool way to go.

But then a couple of Mithrians pulled Pilar out of the entrance to the lava tube and dragged her up to the fire.

"Pilar," I screamed.

One of the Mithrians shoved her to her knees. Then I saw a big dagger flash in Simon's hand.

"What are you doing?" I yelled at him. "I'm supposed to be your sacrifice, not her! Let her go!"

"I think not," he said to me. He turned to his audience again.

"With villainy, Etherea defeated Mithras and he retreated to the underworld. He has waited for thousands of years to ascend. The prophecy says that when Mithras and Etherea are both reborn, the first step in the ascension of Mithras is that Etherea must lose that which is dearest to her. Etherea reborn stands before us now. And as it is written, we shall now take that which is dearest to her."

What? What is this mumbo jumbo about a prophecy?

"Stop this, you big freak!" I yelled. "You're supposed to be sacrificing *me*! That's what all this is about. Can't you even figure out your own stupid prophecy?"

"On the contrary," he said. "The prophecy is quite clear in the *Book of Seraphim*. The first sacrifice is to be that which Etherea holds most dear. Obviously you are quite attached to Ms. Jordan; therefore, Mithras will accept her sacrifice."

"That shows how much you know. Your prophecy is wrong, you idiot. You have the wrong book! Mr. Kim planted a fake in the gallery in Washington and you stole the wrong one!"

For a moment, in the firelight, I could see uncertainty cloud Blankenship's eyes. He'd been waiting years to get to this point, and obviously he didn't want to screw it up. But I couldn't keep the desperation out of my voice, and I could tell he didn't believe me.

"Nice try," he said. "Again, I applaud your bravery. I even admire it." I saw Leikala frown when he said that. She really hated my guts, which is strange, because I'm actually a very nice person. Blankenship was still talking.

"But attempting to deceive me won't work. My scholars have assured me that I have the authentic book in my—"

"Oh, I'm sure they have! In the first place, it's impossible to take you seriously with you wearing that stupid costume. You look like you're ready for trick-or-treat or a *Star Trek* convention. In the second place, what do you *think* you would do to one of your stupid scholars if they dared to tell you your copy was a fake? Mr. Kim tricked you. *He* has the real book!" I knew I shouldn't be blabbing all these details. But he had a knife to my best friend's throat. What else could I do?

"And you expect me to believe that you wouldn't tell any lie to save your friend's life?" He held the dagger closer to Pilar and actually ran it along her throat. Her eyes got wide, but she didn't flinch. I made a promise to myself right then. If it took me the rest of my life, I was going to take this guy down. No matter what it took, no matter where I had to go or what I had to do, Mithras was toast.

"Even if your stupid prophecy was right, you're going about it completely wrong! Take that which is dearest to me? Well, it ain't her. I don't even like her. I mean, look at her hair, for crying out loud. It's like a rats' nest." Pilar's eyes narrowed. Even when you're in a life-and-death situation, you really should never criticize another girl's hair.

"I don't believe you," he said. "Continue with the ceremony!"

"I mean it!" I shouted. "If you think *she's* what's closest to me, then you are crazy! If you wanted to destroy 'that which is closest to me,' then you'd better blow up the nearest Abercrombie & Fitch! Or smash my laptop! Or bump off Ashton Kutcher! All of those things are 'dearer' to me than her!"

Dumb and Dumber were holding my arms, or else I would have charged him.

And then, all of a sudden, the sky around us exploded in a flash of blinding red light.

CHAPTER THIRTEEN

The Boys Are Back in Town

For a minute I couldn't figure out what was happening. We kept hearing and seeing these explosions of red light that filled the pit all around us. Then it hit me. Alex! He'd warned me "there would be fireworks"! He was using the flare gun that Brent had brought to shoot flares all around the pit. It was loud and confusing and a perfect diversion.

This was my chance. Dumb and Dumber had relaxed their grip on me in the confusion. I dropped straight to the ground and jerked my arms free. Then I sprang to my feet and ran at Blankenship. He was looking up at the flares going off and didn't see me coming. I put my shoulder down and ran right into his chest, knocking him to the ground. Pilar spun away. Even though her hands were tied behind her, her feet were free.

"Run!" I yelled at her, and she didn't have to be told twice. She sprinted across the bottom of the pit, toward the lava tube on the opposite side.

I wanted them to have to chase us both, so I started to sprint toward the scaffolding. But I got only a few steps before I felt someone grab my robe from behind. I turned around to see Leikala clutching the gown and digging in her heels.

"Let me go!" I screamed at her.

"No!" she yelled.

I grabbed a handful of the gown as hard as I could and twisted in the opposite direction. The sudden change in balance made her fall to the ground and lose her grip. I sprinted to the scaffolding and started climbing up. I scampered up a few feet and then felt the scaffolding shake. Glancing down, I saw Dumber climbing up after me. I kept climbing as fast as I could. When I was maybe thirty feet from the top, I felt the scaffolding vibrate as the elevator started down from above.

Then somehow a bright light lit up the pit. I heard this loud roaring noise and felt a wind whip up all around us. But I was being cut off from escape and couldn't pay attention to all of that. I was trapped about thirty feet up from the ground, with Dumber gaining from below and the elevator coming down to crush me. My only chance was to see if I could work around to the side, out of the way of the elevator.

I looked down again to see Dumber getting closer. That was my mistake, because as I was trying to move sideways on the scaffolding I missed the crossbar with my foot and stumbled. I tried desperately to clutch at the next crossbar with my hand, but I couldn't reach it. I felt Dumber reach out and snatch my ankle as I fell past him.

I heard Pilar scream. If Dumber let go, I wasn't going to survive the fall. Even if I did, Mithras would have me, and I knew what would happen next. But I could hear Dumber grunting as he tried to hold on to me and keep his grip on the scaffolding. He was hanging off the crossbar at a hard angle. We slipped an inch, then another, and a few seconds later, he let go of my ankle.

In about one and a half seconds, as I floated toward my death, I remembered Pilar telling me about her dream: me in a white robe, falling toward Mithras. She really was psychic. Had that dream been only three days ago? *Good-bye, cruel world*, I thought.

Except that I didn't die. I didn't die because about ten feet from the ground, something stopped me. I felt a huge crushing pressure around my ribs and I stopped in midair with a lurch. Then I heard a familiar voice.

"See what happens when you talk us into leaving school?" Brent said.

Brent! He was strapped into a harness hanging from a helicopter that hovered above the pit. That had been the loud whirring noisy windy bright thing. He had dived out of the helicopter and grabbed me around the waist as I fell. I couldn't believe it. I was so relieved, I wanted to kiss him. Right then, for a second, I felt completely safe. It's funny how things fly through your mind at times like this. It just seemed so cool that Brent was always watching out for me. He was holding me like

I was light as a feather. I didn't realize how strong he was.

"Are you okay?" he said.

"I am now," I said.

The helicopter pulled us up to the edge of the pit and set us on the ground. The elevator had reached the bottom of the pit, and some more of the Mithrians had clambered onto it and were starting back up. Brent set me down, walked over to the control panel, and yanked on a couple of wires. There was a sparking flash and the elevator came to a halt. Now they couldn't get up unless they climbed.

Alex came running up to us, holding the smoking flare gun in his hand.

"Where's Pilar?" he shouted.

"I don't know," I said. "When the flares went off we got separated. She was headed for the lava tube, so maybe she got away."

"We need to find her," he said. He sounded worried.

"Looking for this?" shouted Blankenship from below.

In horror, we watched as two Mithrians walked out of the tube with Pilar in tow. When she got close to the bonfire, we could see that her face looked totally dejected.

"We'll be able to complete the sacrifice after all," he said. He pulled the dagger from his robe and held it aloft. The metal flashed in the firelight.

"No!" shouted Alex. He pushed past Brent and me and started to the edge of the scaffolding like he was going to climb down and take them all on. Brent reached out and grabbed him. Alex tried to struggle free.

"Alex, wait!" I shouted. "Blankenship! Listen to me. Your book *is* a fake. But if you don't believe that, believe this. I know where the missing artifact is on this island. If you harm her in any way, I'll make sure you never get it. I will burn it and throw the ashes into the deepest part of the ocean!"

"You're a very convincing liar, Etherea! But your friend must die. Her death brings Mithras power!"

He raised the dagger. This was it.

"I'll get it for you!" I shouted.

Blankenship lowered the dagger.

"What did you say?" he asked.

"You heard me," I said. "I know where it is. And I can get it. I'll trade it for Pilar. Give me six hours. What do you have to lose?"

Pilar started yelling through her gag.

Blankenship stopped for a moment. Doubt crossed his face. If I had the artifact, that would be impossible to resist. It was the one thing he needed.

"All right," he said finally. "We keep the girl. Return in four hours with the statue or she dies."

"I need at least six hours," I said.

"You have four hours," Blankenship said.

"I need six."

"Four."

"Six!"

"Four." He wouldn't negotiate. I may not have mentioned it before, but I really, really didn't like this guy.

"So if I bring you the artifact, you'll let us go?"

"Oh no, my dear Etherea. That is not the deal at all. You bring me the artifact and *she* lives. I let her go. But you stay with me. *That* is the deal."

Well, I had to say his deal pretty much sucked. But I couldn't think of any other way out of this.

"All right. All right. I'll do it." Pilar was getting all bug-eyed and making noises and shaking her head back and forth. I could tell she hated this plan, but I wasn't going to let her die because of me.

"No tricks, Etherea. We will meet in the valley where you escaped from the compound. If you call the police or try any of your tricks, she dies. You have four hours. Starting now."

He turned and walked away across the floor of the pit. Pilar was being dragged along after him by Dumb and Dumber, and they all entered the lava tube and disappeared. The clearing fell silent. It was almost like they'd never been there at all.

CHAPTER FOURTEEN

Not Much of a Plan as Plans Go

Alex and Brent looked at me. We were all too stunned to say anything for a minute. Then we all started talking at once, even Brent.

"What was all that about the artifact? Did you really find it?" Brent asked.

"Well, no, but Pilar figured out where it is, sort of."

"Sort of? What do you mean sort of? You know where it is, right?" Alex said.

"Well, it was kind of confusing because we were being chased and then she said some weird stuff about a place where Pele walks into the sea and I totally had no idea what she was talking about but I bet we can figure it out."

"*What?* You just said . . ." He was yelling. Alex yelled a lot.

"Alex, enough!" Brent said sharply. He was normally so quiet that his sharp tone startled us. "Rachel, tell us exactly what happened and what Pilar said. As best as you can remember," he said. Quiet, mysterious Brent taking charge in a crisis. Cool.

So I did. I told them everything Pilar had said when she was looking at the map in the observation post. Brent pulled a small flashlight and a map of the island out of his knapsack. He spread it on the ground. I showed him where I thought she'd pointed.

The spot on the map called Pele's Point.

"That's it," I said. "That's the place she was talking about. The relic must be there."

"How do we know?" Alex said. "Maybe she was wrong. We don't have time to be wrong here."

He was right. If we were wrong, then Pilar was going to die. But Pele's Point was all we had. I just hoped it was enough.

Brent pulled out a walkie-talkie and said something into it. A few minutes later the helicopter, which had been circling the area, came swooping back in and landed not too far away from where we stood. Before we got in, I ran back to the van (which the moron Mithrians had left there, unlocked) and grabbed the duffel bag with my phone and cash in it. Then we all hopped aboard the helicopter.

The pilot was a Hawaiian named Kanale. He was a big friendly guy and obviously pals with Brent and Alex. Alex explained that after we'd disappeared they'd hitched back to the hotel, which, they discovered, offered helicopter tours of the island. And the best thing was it could be charged directly to the room, which was on my dad's American Express.

So they had Kanale fly them over the terrain several times, but the jungle canopy was too dense to find anything. (Not to mention the fact that we were hidden inside a mountain.) Finally they told the pilot a little of what happened—that we were missing and we'd been grabbed by some unfriendlies. Kanale agreed to help them.

At last Brent's GPS picked up a signal from our watches, which led them to the pit, where Brent had been just in time to snatch me from the jaws of certain death.

It only took a few minutes by helicopter to get to Volcanoes National Park. We headed for the southern end of the park, where the lava bubbles up out of the ground and runs down into the sea. When the flow is very active, a stream of lava actually shoots out of the side of a cliff and into the water like a molten waterfall. The lava instantly cools when it hits the water and steam rises high into the sky. The cooled lava becomes hard in the water and builds up over time. It is said that the Big Island of Hawaii is growing by a few feet each day as the lava hardens into land.

At night it was beautiful. But I couldn't concentrate on it, as my mind was consumed by thoughts of Pilar being held prisoner by a madman, all because of me. I was twisting and fidgeting in my seat. Alex sat facing me, and Brent sat to my left. Never missing an opportunity to learn something, he was staring intently out the window at the lava flow. All I could think about was how guilty I felt. Once again, I had dragged my friends from the safety of the school and directly into danger.

Maybe Alex was right—I was nothing but a magnet for trouble.

I was so jumpy, I almost screamed when Alex reached out and took my hand. I thought he was going to yell at me to keep still or stay focused or something like that. But he didn't. He held my hand and looked at me. I could see the concern in his face, and then I could tell that even though he was most worried about Pilar he was also concerned about me.

"She'll be all right," he said.

"She might not be," I said.

I looked at him and tried really hard, given the gravity of the situation, to not notice how incredibly blue his eyes were. But they were *so* blue.

"Yes, she will. You don't know her like I do. Pilar is tough. She's smart. She's not going to crack, and you won't either. You don't give yourself enough credit sometimes, Raych," he said. *Did he just call me Raych?* Gulp. He'd never called me that before.

He was still holding my hand, and at this point I was hoping he didn't notice that my palm was getting all sweaty.

"I don't want any credit for anything. I just want her safe," I said.

He gave my hand a squeeze. "I know," he said. "I know."

And he smiled at me. It was a great smile. *Stop thinking about his smile,* I scolded myself. *Your best friend,* his girlfriend, *is in horrible danger.* But Alex's was the Michael Jordan of smiles.

"I don't know what to do," I said.

"You'll think of something."

"I wish I had your confidence."

"You do. You think you're running around with no plan, but you always have a plan. You'll figure something out. That's your gift. You look at a situation, you analyze it, and you act. And I know you'll get us through this. I have no doubt."

He looked away, out the window at the lava glowing below us. But he didn't let go of my hand.

Weird. That's the only word I could use to describe it. All the time I'd been at Blackthorn I'd thought that Alex could barely tolerate my presence. Now he was talking like he actually liked me. The pressure must have been making him crazy.

A few moments later Kanale shouted that we were going to land at Pele's Point. He startled me, and I pulled my hand away from Alex's grip. He just smiled again. *Yikes! Stay focused, Rachel.*

Slightly to the west of the main lava flow was Pele's Point. This was where Pilar had said the statue was hidden. Kanale set the chopper down and we jumped out. Before he took off he shouted at us to be careful.

"You should be okay here, but watch out: The ground around here is funky. Sometimes it'll blow, and before you know it, you'll be surrounded by lava with no way out. I'll keep circling until you call me on the walkie!"

Great. Thanks for the advice. If only I'd packed my lava-proof boots.

Way off in the distance behind us we could hear the hiss of the lava hitting the ocean and the sound of the steam blowing high into the sky. A few hundred feet ahead of us were five very large, irregularly shaped granite pillars that thrust up out of the ground. They looked like oversized monuments or something.

"So," I said, "here, artifact, artifact, artifact!" I was trying to break the tension, but they didn't laugh.

"Okay," said Brent, "if there were island inhabitants when the Romans landed here, this might have been a holy place to them. And perhaps those pillars reminded the Centurions of a Roman temple. It's also not easy to get to. This would be a good place to hide something."

Was it just me or had the normally quiet, taciturn Brent turned into Mr. Blabbermouth? But as usual, when he did say something, it made sense. The question was, where would you hide an artifact in a place like this if you were a Roman on a Hawaiian vacation two thousand years ago?

"But you know what I still don't get?" Alex said. "How could Flavius know about this place? I mean, Hawaii is a long, long way from Rome. It just doesn't seem possible that he could have written what's in the book. He'd have had no knowledge of Hawaii. How could he know what to write?"

Neither of the boys was looking at me. If they were, they would have seen me shudder. I remembered the thing I saw in the hold of the ship that night. I had to believe that Flavius had help in hiding all of his bling bling. He had something or someone telling him everything he needed to know—exactly where to go and what to do.

I figured at this point Alex and Brent needed to know what we were dealing with. So while we searched, I told them everything about that hideous thing I'd seen in the cargo hold. It was the only thing that I hadn't shared with them. Mr. Kim had thought it best to keep it between us. But now was not the time for secrets. If they were going to risk their lives, they needed to know everything.

Brent just nodded when I finished. Mr. Skepticism, on the other hand . . .

"I don't believe any of this for a minute. Supernatural help? Please. Although it does seem like the only possible explanation for how the artifact could be here."

"Yeah, well, speaking of artifact," I said. "We need to find it. According to my watch, we've got three hours and fifteen minutes to get back to the meeting place."

I made an executive decision to start at the center pillar and work our way out. Since they were arranged in a kind of rough star shape, it seemed the best place to start. Brent led the way with his flashlight. But after a few minutes I realized that we were going to fail. The pillars were huge and there was too much ground to cover. The treasure wasn't going to be lying around waiting to be found. There was no big sign with an arrow that said "Ancient Roman Relic Hidden Here." We were going to run out of time. And we might have if I hadn't accidentally discovered the power of Etherea's light.

CHAPTER FIFTEEN

Let There Be Light

It happened when Brent's flashlight battery burned out. We stood there in total darkness. Brent shook his flashlight. It was completely dead. There was some moonlight, so we could see each other a little, but not very well. We stood there in silence, staring at Brent.

He looked up from fiddling with the flashlight.

"What?" he said.

"Nothing," I said. "We're just waiting for you to replace the batteries."

"Yes. Well. I don't have any," he said.

"You don't have any extra batteries? You bring a flare gun and half a secret-agent lab in your backpack, but no batteries?"

"Nope," said Brent.

"Alex, do you have a flashlight?" I said.

They looked at me and then at each other.

"Don't tell me," I groaned. I pointed to Brent's backpack with all the stuff he'd packed into it back at the school. "Are you sure there's not another flashlight in there?" He shook his head.

Appalling. Of course, I had nothing with me, but *I* had an excuse, what with being captured by a supervillain and everything. These guys were just woefully unprepared.

"Can't you use the batteries from something else in your pack?" I said.

"Not the right size," he said.

Brent was still shaking his light, trying to get it to work. No such luck.

In exasperation, I reached out and took the flashlight from his hands.

"Let me see that," I said.

And that's when it happened. As I reached for the flashlight, my hand started to glow. Imagine turning on the headlights of a car and then putting your hand over the top of one. Know how it makes your skin look almost transparent around the edges and makes your fingertips glow? That's what it looked like. My hand began to throb with a weird energy, and when I took the flashlight, a brilliant white light shot out of the flashlight in a bright beam.

I screamed and dropped the flashlight. It clattered across the ground, spinning in all directions, and came to rest a few feet away from me. Then a loud screech seemed to come from it and the beam got brighter and there was a crashing sound as some of the rocks in the path of the beam collapsed and rolled down the side of the pillar in a mini–rock slide. Then the glow of the beam dimmed and the flashlight just lay there shining, looking like a regular old flashlight with a fresh set of batteries. Slowly the glow faded from my hand.

"Whoa," Alex said.

"Did you see that?" Brent asked.

"Rachel, what . . . are you okay?" Alex asked.

"Uh. Yeah. I think . . . I'm not . . . I don't know," I said. Truth was, I felt a little light-headed and dizzy. What the heck had just happened to me? I stood there looking at my hand like it wasn't a part of me.

"What was that?" Alex asked.

"I'm not sure. My hand felt kind of funny, and all of a sudden it was like a big jolt of static electricity shot out of it or something. But it's not like I've never touched a flashlight before. I've probably picked up a zillion flashlights in my life, but I swear to God *that's* never happened. What's wrong with me?" I was clenching and unclenching my fist, hoping like heck that whatever had just happened wouldn't happen again anytime soon. I felt frightened. This was a total freak-out moment.

"Must have been some kind of electrical charge," said Brent. "There's all kinds of heat in the rocks here, not to mention radiant electrical energy. The low-grade electrical field from the flashlight must have caused a spark."

Thank you very much, Dr. Science. But that didn't explain the bolt of light shooting out of the flashlight and knocking the rocks off from the side of the pillars. Or maybe it did—what do

I know? I looked at Alex, who was still staring at me with his mouth open.

Brent walked over to where the flashlight lay on the ground and very gingerly picked it up, like he was expecting it to explode or something. He jiggled it a couple of times and flicked it on and off. It seemed to be working perfectly. The tingling sensation was finally starting to disappear from my hand.

"I don't get this. What happened to me?" I said.

"I think Brent's explanation is probably accurate," Alex said slowly. "We are essentially standing on a live volcano. The heat and the atmosphere can play all kinds of havoc with equipment and stuff. Luckily it seems to have recharged the batteries in the flashlight." He took the flashlight from Brent and waved it around like a wand.

Okay. Fine. Whatever. So nobody really wanted to talk about it. We'd deal with it later.

While Alex swung the light around, it happened to sweep over to where the rocks had shifted. As it passed over the rubble, I noticed what looked like a small opening in the side of the rock.

"Hey, wait a minute," I said. "Shine the light back on the rock slide."

"Why don't you just turn on your hand instead?" he said. Then he and Brent busted out laughing. Comedians.

"Quit goofing around. Look," I said. They followed me over to the opening.

Steam poured from the opening and a mysterious light glowed from within. *Probably some kind of lava pocket*, I said to myself. Couldn't be anything else but lava here. This place was like a Wal-Mart of hot molten rock. But now I had this very strong instinct to crawl into this little hole and look for something—almost like I was being led there. So into the hole we went.

We scrambled through the small opening and found that it turned into a tunnel that led back into the rock. We followed it for maybe twenty yards on a downward slope and wound up in a very large cavern. And there in the middle of the cavern was what I can only describe as a solid wall of light. It shot right up out of the cavern floor and reached all the way to the ceiling. It glowed and pulsed with white energy, and it wasn't transparent so we couldn't see beyond it. It looked almost like a force field that you might see in a science-fiction movie.

"What the heck is that?" Alex said.

"Don't know," said Brent.

"I don't know either, but this must be the place," I said.

"Agreed," said Alex. "Now what?"

The light kept pulsating and shimmering. It was like daylight inside the cavern. I picked up a small rock and tossed it at the light wall. It bounced off and landed on the ground. Okay. What next?

Brent walked up to the wall and put his hand out, but he couldn't push it through the wall. It *was* like a force field. It didn't shock him or anything—it was more like the light turned solid when his hand touched it. He took off his backpack and pulled a little box gizmo out with all kinds of dials and knobs on it. He started pushing buttons and waving it back and forth near the light.

"What is that thing?" I asked.

"Spectroscope," he said. He was concentrating very hard on what he was doing.

"What does it do?"

"Measures light," he said. Give the guy a project and he returns to his one-syllable ways.

Brent took the Spectrowhatsit and ran the machine over my magic light show hand. He looked at the readout and frowned.

"Rachel," he said, "I think you need to try it."

"Try what?"

"Try sticking your hand through the wall of light."

"What?"

He looked up at me.

"Try sticking your hand through the light," he said.

Well, wasn't there something else I could try? Maybe wrestle a lion or something instead? This whole thing with my hand lighting up and this weird wall of light was freaking me out a little, and knowing my luck, if I stuck my hand through that light, it'd come back looking like it belongs to Edward Scissorhands or something.

"You're sure about this?" I said to Brent.

"Yeah. Pretty sure," he said. *Pretty* sure?

"This isn't going to hurt me, is it?"

"Don't know," he said. "Don't think so. Didn't hurt me when I touched it."

So Mr. Science wants me to stick my hand into a wall of weird energy that no one has ever seen before and find out what happens. If I lived through this, these guys were going to be covering my shifts in the kitchen for the rest of the school year.

I didn't have any other ideas, so I reached out with my hand and touched the light. Only, unlike Brent, my hand passed right through. I couldn't see it through the barrier, but it was still attached to my arm and the wall of light hadn't stopped it. Great. You can guess what this means.

"You need to go through," said Brent.

"Hey, maybe we can find some other artifact, like at a flea market or something, and trick Blankenship with it. I mean, it's not like he's ever seen the real thing. How would he know? I think I saw something suitable at Pier One not too long ago. It would look great in a Mithrian temple."

Brent nodded toward the light wall, like it was time for me to get on with it. Whoo boy.

I was back to the nervous babbling, and that was because, inside, I knew Brent was right. I had to go through that wall of light, because somehow I knew that was where the missing relic was and that was the only thing that could save Pilar. No one else could do it. It had to be me. Where was Arnold Schwarzenegger when you needed him?

"Okay," I said, taking a deep breath. "I can do this." I pulled back my hand and looked at it. None the worse for wear. Still had all my fingers. So it wasn't going to hurt me. Scare the bejabbers out of me maybe, but probably not going to be harmful. Except to my nerves.

Alex reached out and put his hand on my shoulder. "Are you sure?" he said.

"I'm sure," I said. He gave my shoulder a squeeze, then

released it and said "good luck." I looked at Brent and winked, and he smiled back at me.

"I'll be right back," I said.

Then I stepped through the wall of light and hit the Mithrian jackpot.

CHAPTER SIXTEEN

Thank You for Shopping at Our Temple

It looked like the pictures of the temple in Kuzbekistan that Mr. Kim had shown us. My eyes immediately went to the golden statue that sat on a pedestal in the center of the room. There were carvings on the walls of Mithras and other drawings and pictures of stuff, but I really didn't have time to study them closely. I needed to get that statue.

The statue was about two feet high and carved in the shape of a bull sitting on its hindquarters, like a dog or cat might sit when it's resting—or getting ready to pounce. Red rubies for eyes and what I guessed must have been silver horns. The rest of the statue looked to be solid gold and encrusted with diamonds and gemstones. Which meant it was going to be heavy.

Out of the corner of my eye I spotted something lying on

the ground near the far wall of the room. Only, it wasn't a some-thing—it was a some*one*. Or it used to be someone. Now it was a skeleton. From the helmet and armor it wore and the large sword that lay next to it, I assumed it was a Roman Centurion. I didn't know much about Roman Centurions, but I had seen *Gladiator* several times and the armor looked just like the stuff that Russell Crowe wore in the movie.

So it was true. Flavius had sent his men all over the world to hide his toys. I concentrated on this fact, because if I could focus on Flavius and his mission from two thousand years ago then I wouldn't be freaked out by the fact that THERE WAS AN ACTUAL SKELETON IN THE ROOM WITH ME! Ick.

I was a nervous wreck and my heart was pounding. I just wanted to get out of there. I was about to take the statue off the pedestal when I remembered something and stopped.

As I like to remind people, Rachel Buchanan is nobody's fool. I had seen all the Indiana Jones movies and I knew there was a very good chance that the statue could be booby-trapped somehow. Once I took the statue off the pedestal, all kinds of bad stuff would probably happen. A giant boulder might come rolling down out of the walls and crush me to death. Maybe all kinds of arrows would come shooting out of the walls and turn me into a pincushion. A giant metal blade might pop up out of the pedestal and whack my arm off. Or machine guns would drop out of the ceiling and spray the room with bullets.

Okay, probably not that last one, since the ancient Romans didn't have machine guns. But some of that other stuff could definitely happen.

I bent down and looked closely at the pedestal. As near as I could tell, it was just carved out of rock. I didn't see any cracks or anything that looked like a secret panel or a hidden vat of acid that would get dumped on my head. Not even a boxing glove on a giant spring. Maybe it wasn't booby-trapped after all. Sure. I bet. So I decided to steal a trick from *Raiders of the Lost Ark*.

I still had the duffel bag from the van slung over my shoulder. I took out my Swiss Army knife, cash, and cell phone and jammed them back in my pockets. I knelt down and started scooping dirt into the bag. The temple floor was covered with a few inches of fine soil, but underneath that was solid volcanic hardened rock. When I ran out of dirt, I added a few temple things—plates, jewels, that kind of thing. I had no idea how much the statue weighed, but I hoped this worked.

I held the duffel bag in one hand by the handles and put my other hand on the statue. I tried to time it just right so that I'd roll the bag onto the pedestal at the same time as I pulled the statue off. Hopefully that would save me from horrible death or disfigurement.

One, two, three. I pulled and rolled, tucked the statue into my chest, and dropped to the ground, curling up into a ball as close to the stone pillar as I could get. I waited for the inevitable explosion or rumbling, slashing, whirring sound that would signify my doom.

Nothing happened. No booby traps. I opened my eyes and glanced around, just to make sure that I hadn't released a giant spider from a hidden cage and it was waiting for me to move before it ate me. Nothing. Whew. I stood up, holding the statue with both hands. It was heavy, but I could carry it. I waited for a second to see if a trapdoor would open beneath my feet or a dragon would fly down from the ceiling and burn me to a cinder. All quiet.

I clutched the statue tightly in my arms and started back toward the wall of light. I had to carry it close to my stomach with both hands. It was awkward and I kind of staggered under the weight of it. I was about halfway across the room when I sensed something was wrong.

For a moment I thought I heard laughter, that same weird guttural laughter that I heard before on the ship. Surely my ears were playing tricks. Then I heard a squeaky, clicking sound. It sounded familiar somehow, but I couldn't place it. Then, a moment later, I felt and heard something go whooshing by my ear. When I turned and looked behind me, I let out a super-duper, grade A, *Scary Movie 3*, *I Know What You Did Last Summer*, *Blair Witch Project* horror-movie scream. I dropped the statue and went immediately into a Tae Kwon Do fighting position.

Because standing there before me was the skeleton of the Roman Centurion, come to life. It was holding its sword in one hand high above its head and was about to bring it crashing down on me.

CHAPTER SEVENTEEN

Outrunning the Boogey Man

The blade came whistling down toward me. I pivoted to my left and tried to sweep the skeleton's legs from under it with my right foot. The sword went swooshing past me and hit the ground where I'd been standing. Too close. The skeleton jumped over my foot sweep and brought the sword around again for another strike. I needed to get out of there. I jumped away again to my left and got the pedestal between me and him. Or was it me and it?

I circled around, keeping the stone pedestal between us. The skeleton kept trying to lunge across the pedestal and stab me with the sword, but I was able to keep out of his reach. I took a quick glance around the room. The only way out that I could see was the wall of light, which I'd come through. I couldn't leave the statue, and every time I tried to circle around toward the light wall, the skeleton would go nuts, coming at me and swinging the sword like a madman . . . er, mad skeleton. There were no doors or secret passages that would get me away from this walking graveyard. I didn't see any weapons lying around, either. A bazooka would have been nice.

Just then I heard the laughter starting again. It was definitely the same laughter that I'd heard that night on the ship. Aside from the fact that an apparently haunted skeleton was trying to kill me, the sound of the laughter totally freaked me out. Then I noticed that the skeleton was changing.

At first the laughter seemed to be coming from all around me, like it was floating on the air. But then it changed and the skeleton's mouth began to move and it sounded like the laughter was coming from it. Also, the empty eye sockets on the skeleton's skull began to glow with a mysterious red light.

Okay. I am so out of here.

I had to figure out a way to distract Skeletor so that I had time to make it through the wall of light. I wondered if the skeleton could follow me or if it wouldn't be able to pass through like Alex and Brent. Not that I cared, because even if it did come through after me I was pretty sure that Alex and Brent could take care of it while I ran screaming for my life.

First things first. I had to get out of there. I was moving to my left when I stumbled. I grabbed at the pedestal to keep from falling and the pedestal kind of rocked back and forth as I landed against it. Aha!

The pedestal was a little taller than waist high and made of rock. It was about two feet in diameter and it was definitely too heavy to lift, but I might be able to use it to distract Bones.

I circled around until I was in just the right spot. All right. Here we go.

"Hey, skinny," I yelled. "Looks like you've been on the Atkins diet for way too long. Eat this!" I made a move forward so that I was close enough to block his sword arm with my left hand. He came toward the pedestal and reached with his other arm to grab me. With my right hand I pushed on the pedestal with all of my might. For a moment it wobbled a little bit, but I dug in and put my legs into it and pushed harder, and it finally went tipping over and crashed into Mr. Walking Carcass. He fell to the ground with the pedestal on top of him.

I turned and sprinted to the statue. I dropped to my knees and lifted it into my arms. Dang, that thing was heavy. I heard the skeleton thrashing and clawing behind me, but I didn't want to waste time looking. I staggered to my feet and started toward the wall of light. The laughter that I'd heard coming from the skeleton seemed to change to a grunting kind of keening sound. I could swear it sounded like an angry bull.

About ten feet away from the wall, curiosity got the better of me. I glanced over my shoulder, only to see the skeleton push the pedestal off itself and spring to its feet, still clutching the sword. It seemed to be moving a lot faster than it should have been able to. And it started toward me with a yell, red eyes glaring.

Feet don't fail me now, I thought. I clutched the statue tightly to my chest and ran. *Must move faster*, I said to myself. *Could move faster if dropped heavy statue*, myself answered. I could hear the skeleton feet clicking across the floor of the cavern, getting closer. I was almost there when I felt a bony hand reach out and grab a handful of my hair. I screamed, jerked my head away, and tumbled through the wall of light and into the outer cavern.

I landed with a grunt right at the feet of Alex and Brent.

"Rachel, are you all right?" Brent said. He knelt beside me, his hand on my shoulder.

Alex took the statue and Brent helped me to my feet.

"Where have you been? What happened to you?" Alex asked.

"In there, trying to get the statue," I said. "Didn't you guys hear all that noise?"

"No, we didn't hear anything. Rachel, you've been gone almost two and a half hours!" Alex said.

"What? That can't be!" I looked at my watch, and sure enough two and a half hours had passed. What the heck? To me it had seemed like I'd been in there for only a few minutes.

"What happened?" Alex asked again, this time with definite concern in his voice.

"It was a Mithrian temple. So I grabbed the statue off this pedestal and then the skeleton of a Roman Centurion came to life and started whacking at me with a sword. So I scrammed out of there."

They both gave me that "okay, she's obviously gone crazy and we'll just smile, nod, and back carefully away" look. Even Brent! Traitor.

"What?" I said.

"Nothing," said Alex. "We're just glad you're okay." He looked at Brent and smirked. So much for believing me about the weird stuff and about how figuring things out was my "gift." Back to being Mr. Big Jerk.

"What are you smirking about?"

"I'm not smirk—"

Right then the wall of light disappeared. One minute it was there, and then poof! It was gone. It startled us all and we kind of jumped. Brent reached out with his arm to where the light wall had been just to make sure it hadn't gone invisible or something, but it was definitely gone.

The cavern looked nothing like I had left it. There was no skeleton, no sword, nothing. No armor from a Roman Centurion. No rubies or diamonds lying around, no markings on the wall. Just an empty cavern.

"But—this isn't right! There was a skeleton right there! And he had this ginormous sword and glowing red eyes. Just like I told you!"

"Told us what?" Alex said.

"What are you? Deaf? That I was chased around by a skeleton in Roman armor, with a sword. It was lying right there!"

"I don't see any skeleton," Alex said.

I wanted to blow my top. I was tired of this constant doubt and having to explain myself every five seconds. If it turns out that I really am the reincarnation of some old goddess, there are definitely going to be consequences for some people. But there was no time for me to lose my cool now. I stopped, took a deep breath, and ran my hand through my hair. I felt something hard and weird, something that shouldn't have been there. It freaked me out, and I started grabbing at my hair to get it out. I pulled out what I guessed was a finger bone from the skeleton. I shrieked and dropped it on the ground in front of us.

"What is that?" Alex asked.

Brent reached down to pick it up. "Looks like a finger bone," he said.

I was still trying to wrap my brain around the incredibly gross fact that I had a centuries old dead guy's finger bone stuck in my hair, yet despite that, I couldn't resist a chance to say I told you so.

"I told you so!" I said. I was madly sweeping my hands through my hair, hoping like crazy there were no other pieces of Roman Centurion anatomy in there. I felt sick to my stomach.

"All right, I'm sorry. Anyway, we need to get to Pilar," Alex said. "Come on!"

We retraced our steps out of the cavern through the tunnel and back outside the stone pillar, then we hiked back to the spot where Kanale had dropped us off. While we were running, Brent called him on his walkie and the helicopter was waiting for us when we got there.

As we traveled, I kept wondering why Flavius would send this statue all the way to Hawaii and then put up a force field that I could walk right through. I mean, what was the point of that? Alex and Brent couldn't pass through it, but I could. Shouldn't Flavius have had better protection for the statue?

And then something occurred to me. What if Mithras didn't have anything to do with the force field? What if the force field was put there by someone to keep other people out and only let a certain somebody in? Like someone who had a beef with Mithras and didn't want him to get that statue?

Someone like the goddess Etherea.

CHAPTER EIGHTEEN

Showdown

Kanale put us down in the lava field outside the Mithrian compound, a short flight from Pele's Point. They were waiting for us. Simon and Leikala and the Stupid twins stood there with Pilar between them. Parked a few yards behind them was their own helicopter. They obviously planned a quick getaway.

We got out of the helicopter and walked toward them. Alex was carrying the statue.

It would be morning soon, and some of the darkness of night was fading. It was light enough for me to see that Simon's eyes got big when he saw the statue. His face contorted in a confusion of greed, excitement, and darkness. What a sicko.

"All right. We have the statue. Let her go," I said.

"Not so fast," Blankenship said. "How do I know that's the

real statue?" Blankenship had changed out of the ridiculous costume and was wearing his jumpsuit again. Still tacky, but not as lame as the giant-horned helmet.

"Oh, for crying out loud," I said. "Like I'd have time to go to the mall and pick up a fake priceless relic. I brought you your statue, now let her go!" In case I haven't mentioned it before, this guy ticks me off. What an attitude.

Blankenship was quiet for a few seconds.

"I think you're up to something," he said.

"You're right. I am. Look behind you!" I shouted, and pointed over Blankenship's shoulder.

Blankenship and the Stupid twins spun around and went into fighting stances. When he realized there was nothing there, Blankenship turned back and glared at me.

"Made you look," I said.

"I am so going to enjoy killing you, you stupid girl," he said.

"Really? Because I thought we could all join hands and sing 'Kum-bye-ya'," I said.

"Really enjoy it," he said.

"By the way, just in case it slips my mind, if you have to choose between the black jumpsuit and the stupid costume with the bull horns sticking out of your head? Go with the jumpsuit. It's much more supervillainy. I mean, that whole cow costume thing? Really, there is no excuse for that kind of fashion faux pas. You looked ridiculous."

"Enough," he said. "Bring me the statue."

"Oh sure," I said. "Where are my manners? Would you like us to just load it into your helicopter for you? We're offering a free delivery special on priceless artifacts this week. What, you think I'm stupid? You give us Pilar and you get the statue." I so wanted to go all Tony Soprano on this guy.

I didn't notice while I was talking so much that Alex was slowly trying to slip behind us back into the darkness, probably thinking he could try to circle around and attack Blankenship from behind. But Blankenship noticed.

"Stay where you are!" He grabbed Pilar, pulled out that big dagger he'd had earlier, and put it to her neck.

"Stop!" I yelled. "Stop it. Calm down. Alex, stop."

I heard Alex make a kind of hissing sound in frustration, but he stopped where he was.

"Okay," I said, "I'm going to bring the statue over. When I start toward you with the statue, you let Pilar go so she can walk toward us. Then you'll have it and me. That's what you want, isn't it?"

"How do I know you won't try to run?" he said.

"You'll just have to trust me. I know you have trust issues, but you can do it."

"Just make sure you don't try anything stupid. If your friends try to follow us, well, that will give me an excellent excuse to dump you into the lava flow." Then he pulled out a very mean-looking gun and pointed it right at me. Gulp. I hate guns.

"Rachel—" Alex started.

"Shh. There's no other way," I said.

"Rachel, don't do this," Brent said.

I lowered my voice so only Brent and Alex could hear me.

"Look, I'll figure out a way to get free. They have to perform a ceremony, so he's not going to do anything to me right away. Wait a few minutes, then try to follow them and get me out of there. And don't worry."

It was weird how I was the one giving orders to the group now. But there was no time for niceties. I had a best friend to save.

I turned to Alex and took the statue from him.

"Be ready," I said.

"Ready for what?"

"I don't know. You're good at this tactical-escape-from-hopeless-situation stuff," I said.

"Be careful."

Blankenship could hear us talking in low tones, and he hollered at me not to try anything sneaky. He actually said sneaky. Loser.

I hefted the statue into my arms. It was heavy for me, though Alex could lift it with no problems. The only way I could carry it was to cradle it in my arms like a baby. I started across the lava field toward Blankenship and his cronies. When I did, he let go of Pilar and shoved her toward us. She started walking toward me. When we met about halfway, she looked at me with a very scared expression in her eyes. Her hands were still tied behind her and her gag was in place. She tried to talk, but I couldn't understand her. Her eyes were nearly bugging out of her head.

"Achel! Moog nat og ris! Jill pill og. Thun!" she said.

I couldn't help laughing. She sounded hilarious.

"Don't worry," I said. "It will be okay."

"No talking!" Blankenship shouted.

I turned away from Pilar and finished my walk to Blankenship's group. Dumber took the statue from me and handed it to Blankenship. Dumb grabbed my arm and twisted it behind my back. Leikala laughed. Did I mention I hate her?

Blankenship took the statue and looked at it like he had been handed the keys to a new Ferrari. He held it up in the air and closed his eyes and kind of swayed back and forth. It was almost like he was dancing to music that only he could hear. For a moment I thought I heard the laughter again, floating through the air and mist around me.

CHAPTER NINETEEN

Taking a Dive

Dumber pushed me toward the helicopter while Blankenship cooed over his statue. Then it happened.

"FREEZE!" someone shouted. I froze. There were lights all over the place, and all of a sudden a bunch of guys in black ninja suits with machine guns popped up out of the ground. At least that's what it seemed like. I had no idea where they'd come from. Then I recognized Mr. Kim's voice.

"Rachel, hit the ground!" he shouted. There were lights flashing all over everywhere and it was confusing and everyone was shouting. I tried to drop to the ground, but Dumber and Dumb grabbed me and left me sort of hanging in midair. Blankenship was shouting for them to carry me to the helicopter, which had started its engines. The pilot must have been on board already. Dumb and Dumber each had one of my arms and were running to the chopper with me between them. Blankenship still had the statue, and Leikala had disarmed one of the agents that had tried to grab her. She gave him a spin kick and he went down.

I saw somebody toss something that was smoking at our feet, but we were running fast and it hit a chunk of lava and bounced away from us. About three seconds later there was the loud pop of a stun grenade that knocked us all to the ground. I saw Blankenship drop his gun, but he wrapped both arms around the statue and held on. Unfortunately it hadn't gone off close enough to us to really stun anybody. Dumb and Dumber scrambled back to their feet. When they reached for me, I spun away and tried to run.

Dumber grabbed hold of my right arm, so I spun around and gave him a palm strike right to the face with my left hand. He grunted and let go of my arm, but before I could get away Dumb grabbed me around the waist from behind, lifted me off my feet, and barreled toward the helicopter door.

He tried to shove me in, but I braced my legs against the door and pushed back as hard as I could. Dumb pushed harder. I held out as long as I could, but my legs buckled and we fell into the helicopter. Blankenship and Leikala scrambled in after us. The shouting and confusion were drowned out now by the sound of the rotors whirring above us. We were starting to lift off.

One of the FBI agents leaped up and tried to jump into the helicopter, but Leikala kicked at his face and he fell to the ground. Now the chopper was up and moving away, and I could see out the open door that Mr. Kim, Alex, Brent, and Pilar were running toward us. But it was too late. Blankenship had me and he was going to get away.

I just hoped that no one started shooting from the ground. Okay, I was probably going to die in a ritual sacrifice ceremony anyway, but I'd rather not go out in a helicopter crash if it's all the same to everybody.

The helicopter had two benches facing each other in the cabin. Blankenship and Leikala sat opposite me where I sat between the Stupid twins. Leikala was smiling a vicious smile while Blankenship just stared at the statue. The doors on both sides of the cabin were still open, and we were moving quickly across the park toward the ocean.

"Where are we going?" I asked.

"Wouldn't you like to know?" Leikala said.

"Haven't we been over this before, Leikala?" I said. "I'll explain it to you again, and I'll use small words. You capture me. I try to escape. This is how the game is played. If you don't tell me where we're going, then I won't know how to get home once I escape from you. That's why I'm asking."

"Your escaping days are over," Blankenship said. He reached under his seat and pulled out a metal case with a hinged lid. Inside the case was hollow with padded foam walls. He took something out of his pocket that looked like a fountain pen or engraving tool or something. He touched this to the bottom of the statue and it made a little beeping sound. Then he put the statue carefully inside the case and closed and latched the lid. He placed it in front of him, like he didn't want it out of his sight.

The chopper was moving fast but staying low to the ground.

Probably wanted to stay off any radar or tracking systems. We were getting close to the ocean. I was guessing that Blankenship had a ship out there somewhere. We'd land and the ship would take off and then no one would ever be able to find us. Once I got on that ship, I didn't think I'd get off it alive.

I looked at the statue case again. Blankenship was sitting right next to the door, with the case between his feet. Dumb and Dumber were no longer holding on to me. Probably daydreaming about their next steroid injections.

"You see, Etherea," Simon said, and then he started droning on and on again about his plan for world domination. About how he knew that this was his destiny and he'd never felt anything in his life like the Power of Mithras, and on and on. But I wasn't listening. I was watching. Leikala, since she'd probably heard this speech a million times before, was looking out the other door. Dumb and Dumber were sitting quietly, hands in their laps, trying to outflex each other. I looked at them, then at the statue case. Just a few more seconds.

I waited until the chopper hit open water. Then I did probably the dumbest thing I've done since I arrived at Blackthorn Academy.

I rocked forward in my seat, and then, as hard as I could, I drove my elbows back into Dumb and Dumber's faces. I hit them both square and felt the satisfying crunch of noses beneath my elbows. Before they could even let out a scream, I lurched out of my seat, grabbed the handle of the statue case, and dived through the helicopter door toward the open water below.

CHAPTER TWENTY

All Wet

Though I really hated her, I have to give her credit, because
Leikala was quick. She was moving toward me even as I jumped
through the door, and she managed to grab my foot. So there I
was, hanging upside down out of a helicopter for the second
time that night. Only, this time the weight of the statue was
pulling me down and Leikala wasn't about to let go. The doorway wasn't big enough for Blankenship or the Stupid twins to
reach through and help her, though they were trying. The
statue kept getting heavier, and I felt like I was going to break
in two.

"I'll drop it!" I screamed.

She still didn't let go. I tried to kick at her with my free foot
but couldn't get the right angle. I felt like my back was breaking.

I figured I had one shot. The chopper had stopped moving forward and now hovered in place. Blankenship must have told the pilot to go higher, figuring I'd be too scared to jump. No time to mess around now. With a shout, I switched the handle of the case to one hand and at the same time started swinging it back and forth in my right hand. Then, on the swing back, I used the momentum that gave me to rise up at the waist like I was doing a sit-up and grab a handful of Leikala's long, perfectly styled, coal-black hair and yank as hard as I could. She screamed and let go of my foot, and I thought about how good it felt to yank her hair like that as I let go and fell to the water below.

The helicopter was probably only ten or fifteen feet above the water, but I was still completely unprepared for the force with which I hit. Ten feet is not all that high, not as high as some high divers in swimming competitions. But they know what they are doing, and are ready and going into the water the correct way. I had the statue case in my hand, and luckily that broke the surface of the water first, but it still knocked the wind out of me.

All the air rushed out of my lungs and I sank, sank, sank below the surface of the water. I thought I was going to pass out, but I kept telling myself not to. I let go of the statue case because it was pulling me down. I hoped it wasn't too deep here so we could find it later. My lungs were killing me and I needed air. I couldn't tell which way was up and I didn't know what to do. I needed to breathe. I was going to drown.

Then all of a sudden I felt something grab my robe. The

water was dark and I couldn't see, so I had no idea who it was. Could be a shark, for all I knew. But I was being pulled in a direction I hoped was the surface. I heard somewhere that sharks sometimes toy with their victims before eating them. That would be just my luck. Grabbed by a shark with a sense of humor.

Then suddenly I broke through the surface. I could breathe. I sucked in a huge lungful of air. When I could make sense of what was going on, I noticed that the helicopter was hovering overhead and there was a bright light shining on me. Leikala was treading water next to me. What do you have to do to get rid of this witch?

"You're coming with us!" she shouted.

"No way. Get away from me!"

"Simon is very angry!"

"Get used to it!" I said.

She grabbed hold of a harness that had been lowered from the helicopter. I could see the lights of the shore off in the distance. I twisted away from her and started to swim.

I spent a lot of time on the beach with my friends when I was in California. I'm not a jock and I hate to exercise, but I am a good swimmer and I like the water. Of course, I wasn't crazy about swimming through dark, scary water, most likely full of sharks, while a supervillain hovered in a helicopter above me, but we have to accept life with all of its shortcomings.

I heard Leikala curse me, and she splashed back in the water to come after me. The spotlight from the chopper swiveled to follow me.

I held my breath and went down under the water. From there I could see the area of light that was outlined by the chopper's searchlight. I swam away from it until I couldn't hold my breath anymore and then I hit the surface, about ten yards out of the light circle. The light started to play over the surface of the water like they were trying to find me. I took a quick breath and dived again, kicking with all of my might and staying under as long as I could. This time when I surfaced I was even farther away from the light, moving parallel to the shore. They were moving toward shore, because they thought I'd be heading in that direction.

I watched as the light played along the surface, and when it started to come back in my direction, I dived again and swam away. Under the water, I shucked off the robe. In all the excitement I hadn't even realized I was still wearing it. But it was white and would make me easier to spot in the water. For as long as I could, I kept diving and swimming, diving and swimming, putting distance between the helicopter and me. Swim. Dive. Swim. Dive. When I was about fifty yards away from the light circle, I started to angle back toward shore. I switched to a backstroke so that I could make progress toward the shore without losing sight of the chopper.

I looked up at the sky, which had gone moonless but was still full of stars. The ocean felt as warm as bathwater. If it weren't for the fact that a crazy person wanted to kill me—and the fact that I once watched a Discovery Channel documentary about how sharks like to feed at night—it would have been downright enjoyable. It was going to get light soon. I hoped they gave up looking for me before the sun came up and they could spot me in the water.

I kept pushing toward the shore, but it had to be a couple of miles away. I turned to watch the helicopter make an ever-widening arc. They had clearly lost track of me, and I knew that wouldn't be making Blankenship happy right now.

Then I saw Leikala come up out of the water and the cable that was attached to the harness pull her back into the chopper. The light went out and the helicopter headed out to sea at blistering speed. No statue. No me. They were taking off. I wondered why.

I started swimming in a straight line toward shore—as fast as I could, but quietly, in a way that hopefully would not have me resembling a tasty shark treat.

After a while I stopped to tread water, trying to rest a moment and catch my breath. That's when I saw three blinking lights coming toward me. More helicopters. More Mithrians? Two of the helicopters went by and one stopped above me. I looked up into the searchlight and waved, hoping like heck it was Mr. Kim.

Right then I felt something hard and scaly brush against my leg, and a few feet away I saw a dark dorsal fin break the surface of the water.

CHAPTER TWENTY-ONE

After This, Kitchen Duty Will Be a Vacation

I held still. But I couldn't hold completely still because then I would sink. I had to tread water or go under. I remembered from the Discovery Channel documentary that if there were sharks around you were supposed to stay calm and not thrash around in the water. Of course, it is very easy for the perfectly safe narrator of a shark documentary to say, "Remain calm and do not thrash around," because the narrator of the shark documentary is not IN THE WATER WITH THE SHARKS!

I kept my eye on that dorsal fin. It moved around me and around me, circling closer. I was concentrating on the shark so hard that I forgot about the helicopter hovering right over me.

Then something hit me on the shoulder and I thought that was it. A shark was going to eat me. I let out an involuntary scream and started thrashing in the water—exactly what you're not supposed to do. But it wasn't a shark. It was a harness attached to a cable from the helicopter. I shot into that harness like my hair was on fire, and it pulled me up and out of the water. I looked down and saw the dorsal fin cut through the water right where I had been just moments before.

A few seconds later I was in the cabin, and there were Alex, Pilar, Brent, and Mr. Kim. Mr. Kim waved to the pilot and the chopper turned to head back to shore.

"Well, it is about time," I said. "I had to jump out of a stupid helicopter and there was a shark! What took you so long?"

"Rachel, are you injured?" Mr. Kim said.

"No. Apart from the fact that I was just about to be shark food!" Mr. Kim pulled a blanket from under his seat and I wrapped myself in it.

"How did you find me?" I asked.

"Your watch," said Brent, smiling as he held up the small GPS that he had used to track the signal from my watch. He had LoJacked me all the way to the middle of the ocean!

"Thanks for coming to get me, guys," I said. Brent and his beautiful watches.

All of a sudden I was exhausted. All of the adrenaline and everything left me all at once and I felt like I could sleep for days.

"Are you sure you're okay?" Mr. Kim asked.

"Well, if you don't count being waterlogged, almost killed, captured by a really bad guy, and the fact that I haven't seen *Gilmore Girls* in months, I'm fine."

"I'm sorry," said Mr. Kim. "Gilmore girls? Are they friends of yours?"

"No, they're not . . . they're on TV . . . it's a . . . Oh, never mind. Anyway, I managed to pull the statue out of the chopper with me. It can't be too far from here."

"Brent?" said Mr. Kim.

Brent was looking at some other gizmo he'd pulled from his backpack. It started beeping.

"Got it," Brent said. He gave Mr. Kim some numbers that didn't mean anything to me.

"What the . . . ," I said.

Mr. Kim whipped out a handheld radio and spoke into it for a few minutes. He was giving someone coordinates on where to look for the statue. I heard someone answer back that they had lost sight of the Mithrian helicopter and would fly back and retrieve the statue while the other chopper continued the search for Blankenship.

Mr. Kim finished his conversation and returned the radio to his pocket.

"I'm relieved that you are okay," he said.

I nodded.

"Of course, there are a few things we need to discuss. Such as your unexcused absences from school. But first you should rest." He said it in a nice way, but what he really meant was "You are in so much trouble you can't begin to comprehend how many extra push-ups this will add up to."

The chopper finally touched down in a large parking lot near the harbor back in Hilo. It wasn't too long before another helicopter flew up and landed next to us. An FBI agent in a wet suit hopped out of the chopper holding the statue case, which he handed off to Mr. Kim.

"It was right there waiting," he said. "Water was only about thirty feet deep. We got it up in no time."

Mr. Kim thanked him and took the statue case.

"How were you able to find it so fast?" I asked.

"We have Brent to thank," he said. "While you were flying to the meeting with Simon, he attached the tracking chip from his watch to the statue so we were able to track it with his GPS unit. Those chips are the newest technology, and they hadn't been in the water long enough to damage them yet." I looked at Brent, and he just kind of shrugged. The guy was definitely a quick thinker.

"We must move the statue to a safe place," Mr. Kim said. "I have made arrangements to use the vault at the Bank of Hilo until we can move it safely off the island. I would like you all to accompany me there."

"Mr. Kim," I said, "if it's all the same to you, I'd like to go back to the hotel now. I'm just really, really beat." Mr. Kim looked like he was going to argue with me, but when he saw how tired I was he relented.

"Of course, Rachel, you've been through a lot. We will drop you at the hotel and the others can accompany me to the bank. I'll fill in the others over dinner, and we'll talk when you're rested." Oh man. The dreaded "we'll talk" speech.

We loaded into a nearby van. In twenty minutes we were back at the Royal Hawaiian. I hopped out, they drove off, and I staggered up to my room. There I emptied my pockets and set everything on the dresser. I took off my watch and set it on the nightstand by the bed. I really wanted a shower.

I let the glorious hot water flow over me for what seemed like an hour. It wasn't until I was finished and starting to dress that something started to bother me. Something about Blankenship and that statue.

As I brushed my teeth, it hit me. I remembered Simon taking that little penlike thing out of his pocket and marking the bottom of the statue. But I didn't think that was a pen. I think he attached something to the statue so he could find it in case he was ever separated from it. And nobody else knew about it, except me.

I was walking back into the room to get my watch and beep the others when I heard a soft knock on the door. I thought it was probably housekeeping.

So you can imagine my surprise when I opened the door and ran right into Leikala.

CHAPTER TWENTY-TWO

Like a Bad Penny, She Keeps Turning Up

She wasn't expecting me, and I think I actually startled her. I shrieked in surprise, and she lunged for me. I jumped back into my room and slammed the door. I could hear her pounding, but she couldn't make too much noise because that would attract attention.

"Come out here!" she shouted.

"Don't you know we voted you off the island?" I yelled through the door. "I'm calling security!"

I ran to the phone and punched the button for the front desk. Nothing happened. No dial tone. They must have shut off the hotel's phone system somehow. They probably sent Leikala up alone, figuring she could take me out without attracting attention. What to do?

My only option was the balcony outside our room. I grabbed my cash and Swiss Army knife off the dresser and ran to the balcony door. Looking down, I didn't see anyone that looked like they were watching my room. We were on the second floor, so it wasn't that much of a drop. Our room faced the parking lot, but there was a little area of landscaping with plants and bushes down below. If I climbed over and hung from the side, I could probably land safely. Of course, the smart thing might be to stay where I was and holler for help, but there could have been more Mithrians about and I didn't want to attract any unwanted company.

I swung up and over the railing, then let go and dropped to the ground.

I had to think for a minute. I needed to get out of here quickly. Once Leikala let them know that I was still free, they'd come looking for me around the back.

I lifted my wrist to call the others with my watch, then realized I'd left it on the nightstand in the room. Dang! I'd never make it to the beach in time. I was sure Leikala or the Stupid twins would be coming around the side of the hotel any minute. My best option was to hide in plain sight.

I ran quickly down the sidewalk to the first door that led back into the hotel, toward the lobby. I didn't see anyone that looked like a Mithrian—just a bunch of hotel employees and tourists milling about doing hotel employee and tourist stuff. Of course, any one of them could be a Mithrian, but I was going to have to take a chance.

I scooted across the lobby, stopping at a table in the center to grab a free copy of *USA Today*. From the far corner of the lobby, I could see the hotel entrance and the hallway entrances that led off it. I sat in a chair, put the newspaper up, and started pretending to read it. I was wearing my tennis shoes, shorts, and a T-shirt, so I looked like any regular Hawaiian vacation visitor.

I kept reading the Life section of the paper and watching the lobby. Hmm. Jennifer Lopez is getting married. *Again.* Like that's news. Kelly Clarkson had a new album coming out. I'd have to make sure I got one the next time we took a mall trip from the Academy. Which would, of course, be the *first* time.

Then it happened. Leikala came out of one hallway and the Stupid twins came out of the other. They met on the far side of the lobby. They were having an animated discussion. Leikala smacked Dumber in the head. He cowered in fear a little bit. I ducked down behind the newspaper and tried to keep an eye on them, while staying inconspicuous.

Just then, the hotel van delivered a bunch of new hotel guests from the airport and the lobby filled up with about twenty more people. It got noisy and busy. From watching them it was obvious that Leikala and the Stupids were frustrated and didn't know what to do. Finally they left through the front door. I peered through one of the glass doors and saw them get into a car across the parking lot.

I hustled out the front door and hopped into one of the waiting taxis.

I told the driver to follow that car. I've always wanted to say that in a taxi! The driver said *"Mahalo"* and pulled out of the hotel entrance.

We drove into Hilo. I had a good idea where they were going. The statue was in the bank vault, and I was pretty sure that Simon had a plan to get it out. Next to me, it was probably the thing he wanted most on this island, and I didn't think he'd leave without getting his hands on it.

Sure enough, after cruising up and down several streets, Leikala's car pulled down an alley across the street from the First National Bank of Hilo. I had the taxi driver pull over to the curb and we waited. A few seconds later, Leikala and the Stupids came out of the alley. Leikala was carrying a gym bag over her shoulder.

It was early Sunday morning, so the bank was closed and the street was empty. Leikala and the Stupids walked up to the bank door. Hilo is kind of a quiet town, and this part of it was mostly offices, so there weren't any people milling about. I watched as Leikala took some stuff that looked like Play-Doh out of the gym bag and shoved it onto the door all around the lock. She and the Stupid twins stepped back from the door a few feet and then all of a sudden the stuff on the door turned a really bright color like it was burning or something. Then it flamed out and the door popped open. There was no noise or explosion or anything. Leikala and the Stupids were through the door and into the bank in seconds. If they had more of that burny stuff, they'd be inside the vault and have the statue in no time.

While all of this had been going on, the cabdriver had been reading a magazine. I told him to get on his cell phone or radio and get the cops, tell them there was a robbery in progress at the bank.

I gave him $50 from my cash and told him if he could find Mr. Kim and bring him here as quickly as possible, he could have another $50. I hopped out of the cab, and he drove off with a quick *"Mahalo."* I hoped he could find them. I hoped they could get back here fast. I hoped that Leikala and the Stupids had just decided to open a bank account with free checking and that's why they went into the bank.

I started down the street to the bank. The First National Bank of Hilo was a four-story building with concrete steps that led up from the street to the front door. I hustled up and peered through the door. I could see the empty lobby inside, but there was no sign of Leikala or the Stupids. They were probably breaking the statue out of the vault right now. I kept waiting to hear sirens or some kind of sign that someone was coming. But I heard nothing. Somehow they must have gotten around the alarm system. Or else it must be a big night for crime in Hilo and all of the police were busy.

I pulled open the door and walked into the lobby, which was of course deserted. Most of the windows were tinted, so it was darker inside. I stopped for a moment to listen, but I didn't hear anything. I was starting to get a little nervous. I couldn't keep count of the number of too-dark, scary places I'd been to since I'd come to this school, and let me tell you, it was starting to get a little old. I would have liked to go back to California and tell the judge who sent me to Blackthorn that all these scary places I'd been climbing and crawling through in the last couple of months were not doing anything to help my rehabilitation. They were succeeding only in scaring the bejabbers out of me.

Off to my left was the tellers' counter, and off to the right was a row of desks that ran down the length of the building. Toward the back and behind the tellers' counter, I could see a hallway that I guessed led to the vault.

Okay. I could do this. Deep breath.

I started down the aisle between the counters and the desks, walking slowly toward the back. Trouble was, I had no idea what to do next. If Leikala and the Stupids were back there stealing the statue, I hadn't a clue what I could do to stop them. It wasn't like I could use my novice martial arts skills to take them out. I didn't have a weapon. I supposed I could try to make a citizen's arrest. Somehow I didn't think they would take me seriously.

I crept cautiously across the lobby, trying to keep my nerves under control. Any second I expected Leikala or Dumb or Dumber to pop up from behind one of those desks and grab me.

I crept down the little vault hallway, past rows of safety-deposit boxes. It was darker back in this part of the bank, but there was still enough light to see where I was going. Something was telling me that this wasn't going to end well.

Finally I made it all the way to the back of the hall, where sure enough the vault door stood open. I could see that a hole had been burned through the steel door where the lock had been. Whatever that stuff was must be powerful. It must have taken a lot of it to burn through a door this big.

I walked right up to the vault door and stopped again to listen. I still couldn't hear anything. It was totally quiet. So I reached up high on the door and pulled it open. If that stuff Leikala was using could burn through steel, I for sure didn't want to get it on my hands. The door was heavy, but I pulled it open as hard as I could and yelled, "AHA!"

The vault was empty.

No one was there. And neither was the statue. There were a bunch of small drawers and cabinets along the walls, none of which looked big enough to hold the statue. And the rest of the vault was completely empty. They had the statue. But the bigger question was where they had gone. I had come into the bank right after them. They couldn't have gotten into the vault, taken the statue, and fled the bank that fast. They couldn't have just disappeared. My guess was they were still in the building somewhere.

I left the vault and ran back down the hallway. This was a four-story building with no back entrance that I could see. I was going to have to search the whole place. *And by the way,* I thought, *where are the police?* It seemed like the cabbie had called them hours ago.

I didn't have to wait long for an answer. As I cleared the hallway, I found the police. The only trouble was, they were all shouting "FREEZE!" And every single one of them was pointing his gun at me.

CHAPTER TWENTY-THREE

Unjustly Accused Again

I put my hands straight up in the air. "Don't shoot!" I shouted. *Please don't shoot.* Nice policemen. No need to get excited.

"Down on the ground, NOW!" There was one cop doing all the yelling. He was in front of the other policemen, who had crowded into the lobby.

"You don't understand," I said. "Something priceless has been stolen. I think the thieves—" I didn't get a chance to finish. He yelled at me again.

"Lady, shut up. Put your hands on your head and get down on the ground," he said.

So much for Hawaiian hospitality.

I realized that if I didn't do what he said, I'd never be able to catch Leikala and the others. So I put my hands on my head and dropped to my knees. The cop who'd been yelling at me holstered his weapon, took hold of my wrist, and put handcuffs on me. When I felt them snap shut on my wrists, I wanted to scream. The cop pulled me to my feet and started pushing me toward the door.

"You don't understand. I'm not the one you want. The robbers are still in the building somewhere. You have to search it before they get away."

"Save it," he said.

There was nothing I could do. There were about ten cops in the lobby. I'd never get away from them. I was going to be taken into the station. That meant Leikala would get away. I hate losing. And I *hate* police stations.

We went out of the bank lobby into the foyer and down the steps to the street. All the way down the steps I was giving the cop an earful about the big mistake he was making.

"They're still in there! Go back! Capture them! You'll get a big promotion and your name in the paper!" I yelled. He ignored me, probably thinking I was high or something.

Nothing else worked, so I relied on one of my favorite tricks from when I was a kid. I did a dead drop straight to the ground, landing on my butt.

"Somebody listen to me!" I screamed. "I'm fifteen freakin' years old. Do I look like a bank robber?"

"If you don't stand up right now—" the cop was saying.

"Let her go, Sergeant," I heard a voice say.

I scrambled back to my feet and looked around. A very large Hawaiian man in a suit stood next to the cop who'd captured me.

"Detective . . . we caught her red-handed, coming out of the vault!" the cop protested.

"I'm telling you I'm innocent! I demand to be released! I want an attorney and my phone call! Right now!" I had worked my way up to a full head of steam.

"Miss Buchanan, I'm Detective Wanake. Come with me, please," he said.

He took a key from his belt and unlocked the cuffs. I turned and gave the cop who'd arrested me one of the best stink-eyes of my life. "I told you I was innocent! You need to search that building right now. There are actual real criminals in there!" I said.

The cop just looked at me with a blank face.

The detective took me down to where Mr. Kim and the gang were waiting beside a squad car, then went back to the cops.

"Let me guess," I said. "Former student?"

"Correct," said Mr. Kim. "Excellent observation. Tell us what happened."

"We need to search that building! They've got to still be in there."

As we started back toward the bank, I told them what had happened. "The vault is empty. They must have the statue. You've got to convince them, Mr. Kim."

Just as I said that, most of the cops that were standing around suddenly sprinted to the squad cars, taking off in a squeal of tires. Detective Wanake came running back to us.

"Mr. Kim," he said, "I'm afraid there is an emergency across town. We have a report of a gas-main break in a residential neighborhood, and my men are needed to evacuate the residents. I'm leaving a man here to guard the bank door, but we will need to speak to your student later."

"Danny," Mr. Kim said. "I think you need to search the bank building."

"No time. My men are needed elsewhere. We will return as soon as we can."

He didn't even wait for a response, just turned and ran to a car and sped off. In a few seconds every cop was gone except for one young policeman who stood by the front door.

"Don't you think it's a pretty big coincidence that just a few minutes after the statue is taken from the bank vault, there's a big emergency across town?" I said.

"It does seem somewhat unlikely," Mr. Kim said.

"So what are we going to do?" I said.

"You will remain here, with the others, while I search the building," Mr. Kim said.

Before I could even argue, he sprinted up the stairs and past the cop into the building. He was very fast for a man of his age, and probably decided to run quickly so that I wouldn't have time to wear him down with an argument.

"This is no good," I said aloud. "The building is too big for one person to search. They could escape before the cops get back! Guys—" I started.

"Save it. You want us to help search, we'll do it," said Alex.

"You will?" I said, stunned. I was expecting to have to go through another big explanation about why we needed to disobey Mr. Kim again, because though his intentions were in the right place he didn't see the big picture and yada, yada, yada. Alex had caught me a little off guard.

"We don't know what floor he's on," Alex said. "Rachel and I will take the top floor and work down. Brent, you and Pilar start on the first floor and work up. We'll meet in the middle."

They nodded, and we took off up the steps.

The cop guarding the door looked at us.

I pulled my cell phone from my pocket and held it up to him.

"Mr. Kim thinks they're getting away—he wants you to cover the back door! We'll guard the front! Hurry!" I shouted.

The cop hesitated for a second, but I waved the phone at him, encouraging him to go. It worked. He sprinted down the steps and around the back of the building. Ha. Wouldn't he be amused when he found out there *was* no back door.

We split up. Alex and I went into the stairwell and cautiously made our way to the fourth floor. We didn't see any sign of Leikala or the Stupid twins. Maybe they got out through a window or some other way. But how had they done it? And why hadn't they set off any alarms? These crooks could really be infuriating.

We stepped out from the stairwell onto the fourth floor. It was full of desks and cubicles. A long row of cubicles ran down the center of the floor, making an aisle on either side. Alex took the left and I took the right, and we slowly made our way down the floor. There is something very creepy about being in a deserted office building. I half expected Freddy Krueger or the Predator to hop out at me. If I'd known that I was going to end up chasing an evil supervillain around the world, I would have watched a lot fewer scary movies growing up.

We made it to the back of the floor and still hadn't found them.

"What are we going to do if we do find them?" I said as we headed back into the stairwell.

He thought for a few minutes. "There are three of them, right?" he asked.

"Yes. Leikala and the two Stupid twins. Both of them are big and very strong. The darker-haired one is left-handed, and the one that has slightly lighter-colored hair has a gimpy right knee thanks to one of my best-ever front kicks. Not to mention he's all beat up because Pilar whupped him good. Oh, and I might have messed up their noses pretty bad. They're dangerous and mean, and I think they're really ticked off at me."

"I'm not surprised," Alex said. "You tend to have that effect on people."

I spun around ready to give him a sharp retort, but his eyes were sparkling. He was teasing me. And I hate to admit it, but I kind of liked it.

But I didn't get a chance to think about it much, because right then he started talking about Pilar.

"Man, Pilar is something," he said. "I can totally picture her smacking that guy around."

"What do you mean I 'have that effect on people'?" I said.

"I think it's pretty self-explanatory. You have a way of getting under other people's skin. Blankenship is so frustrated with you, it's unbelievable."

Was that a compliment?

He laughed when he saw the look on my face, and then, very quickly, he reached out, grabbed both of my hands in his, and gave them a quick squeeze. A very nice, friendly little squeeze that was thrilling and confusing all at the same time. Then he let go of my hands and pushed past me into the stairwell. I was still standing there like a big doofus, and he turned around and smiled at me.

"Coming?" he said.

"Uh . . . yeah . . . I mean, yes." I tried to pull myself together and follow him. I remembered how he'd treated me on the helicopter on the way to Pele's Point. I had to say I couldn't figure him out sometimes. I mean, I thought he hated my guts most of the time, but now it sounded like he was warming up to me a little. But he also obviously cared a lot for Pilar.

Oh dear God. Did I have a crush on this guy? Maybe I'd just go straight to the roof and throw myself off.

"Alex, can I ask you something?" I said. I realized that this wasn't the best time in the world to be dealing with this kind of stuff, but what the heck.

He stopped and looked at me. "Sure," he said. "What?"

"Do I really annoy people that much?" I said.

"Yes," he said. He saw the hurt look on my face and quickly continued. "But that's also part of your gift. You don't quit, Rachel. You like to act all uninterested and like you're ready to walk away any minute. But you're not a quitter. You're going to see this through to the end. You might annoy us—me sometimes, but it's only because you're persistent. The most persistent person I've ever met."

"Persistent is good, right?" I asked.

Alex laughed. "Yeah, it's good."

Hmm. It was funny. Alex thought he had me all figured out. Maybe he did. I mean, I never thought that he was even aware of me except as someone he wished would just disappear. And I thought he was just a muscle-head who cared only about studying, working out, and breaking boards in the *do jang*. But maybe I was wrong about him. Maybe there was more to him than just the buff-ness and the attitude.

I must have had a blank look on my face while I tried to process this.

"Hello. Rachel? Are you still here?" he said. "We're trying to catch some bad guys here, remember?"

He was right. I needed to focus. As much as I wanted to continue this conversation (or did I?), now was not the time.

"If there's a scuffle, do you think you can hold your own with Leikala until Mr. Kim and the others get here?"

"Not a chance," I said. "She's way better than me. She has the skills and she's not afraid to use them. I'd last about three seconds in a fight with her."

"You're better at Tae Kwon Do than you think. You've improved a lot in the last two months."

"I have?"

"Yeah, you're getting better at it. So my plan is, if we find them, try to keep Leikala occupied while I handle the twins. Don't worry about trying to take her down or anything. Just get close enough to her to feint and parry, and don't let her get her hands on you. Keep her busy. Make her mad if you can. That should be easy for you. When I have the twins down, I'll come help."

"Those guys are huge, Alex. What makes you think you can take them?"

"All I can do is try. Like the oath says, 'have perseverance in battle.' Hopefully my speed and quickness will compensate for their size and strength."

"That's your plan?" I said.

"You have a better idea?"

The trouble was, I didn't. If Mr. Kim didn't hear a commotion and come to help, we were on our own.

We started down the steps to the third floor, when I heard a familiar noise.

"Do you hear that?" I said.

Alex stopped to listen. "A helicopter. They're on the roof!"

We sprinted up the stairs, bursting through the door and onto the roof. On the far end, the Stupid twins and Leikala stood watching a helicopter lower a ladder toward them.

"Come on!" Alex shouted, and he took off sprinting toward them. Did I mention I wasn't crazy about his plan?

The roof of the bank was covered in a gravel surface. There were all kinds of metal ventilation covers and satellite dishes and other obstacles spread all around it. Alex was fast, and though I'm fairly quick myself, I had to run hard to keep up with him.

Leikala and the Stupids heard our shout and turned to see us running toward them. The ladder was only a few feet from them now. Dumber put the case with the statue down on the ground, and he and Dumb turned to face Alex's charge. Leikala shouted something at them, but it was hard to hear with the noise from the helicopter.

Alex reached Dumb first. He skidded to a stop on the gravel surface of the roof and went into his crouch. Dumb took a swinging roundhouse punch at Alex, which he dodged easily. Dumb's momentum carried him nearly past Alex. Almost faster than I could see, Alex spun behind Dumb and took him down with a kick to the back of his knee. Dumb crumpled, and Alex put a vicious front kick to the side of Dumb's head and he went all the way down. That was definitely going to leave a mark.

I saw Dumber come at Alex swinging, but by now I was near Leikala. She yelled at Dumber to forget Alex and get the statue on the chopper, but he ignored her. I grabbed the statue case and turned to run. Leikala came after me like she was a Doberman and I had a pork chop tied to my butt. I got only a few steps before she tackled me and the statue case went skittering across the roof. I went down hard on the gravel, and it hurt. Leikala was screaming at me and trying to grind my face into the gravel. I was definitely getting tired of this chick.

I pushed up with my arms with all my might and managed to roll over so I was on top of Leikala, then spun away from her. I stood back up, and she did one of those fancy martial arts backflip things and leaped to her feet.

She came at me, but I darted back so she couldn't reach me. Then she seemed to remember what she was supposed to be doing. She stopped and turned, looking for the statue.

The helicopter was hovering above us still, whipping up all kinds of dust and gravel and making it hard to see. Off to my left I could see Alex and Dumber going at it. Dumb was still down on the ground. Alex looked to be holding his own.

Leikala grabbed the case with the statue in one hand and with the other leaped up and grabbed one of the ladder rungs. The chopper started to move slowly away. Oh no you don't.

I sprinted toward Leikala, jumped up, and grabbed her around the waist, holding on as tight as I could. She couldn't do anything, because one hand held the ladder and the other held the statue and she wasn't going to let go of either. The chopper hesitated for a moment as if the pilot wasn't sure what to do, then it started to move again.

I freed one arm and punched her as hard as I could in the ribs. She groaned but didn't let go. The helicopter was hovering over the roof; the pilot seemed afraid that if they moved away, we might fall and then the statue would be gone. I punched Leikala in the ribs again, but I really couldn't hit her very hard. I was getting tired trying to hold on to her with one arm and punch with the other. We started spinning around and around like we were going to land.

I wondered where Mr. Kim and the others were. Now would be an excellent time for them to show up. It seemed like we'd been up here forever, but I knew in reality it had been less than a minute. And by the way, I was really sick of helicopters. I had already jumped out of one on this trip, and I had no desire to do it again.

Leikala was screaming at me to let her go. I screamed back

at her that ignoring her inner child was causing her to act out needlessly. She swung the statue case and drove it up into my back. It hurt like the dickens and I couldn't hang on any longer.

I fell to the roof with a thud. I looked up and saw Simon peering over the side from the cabin. When he saw that I was down, he laughed.

I staggered to my hands and knees. I looked around and saw that I had landed right next to one of the satellite dishes on the bank roof. There was a coil of black cable next to the dish and what looked to be a bracket that might once have held another dish.

The chopper would clear the roof in a few seconds. I grabbed the end of the cable and ran toward Leikala. As she pulled away, I coiled the cable around her legs as fast as I could. The chopper was still moving, but now she was stuck. She had no choice now—she had to let go or she'd be pulled apart by the cable. She screamed and let go of the ladder. The chopper rocked in the air when her weight was released. She hit the side of the roof right on the edge and, still holding the case with the statue, went tumbling over the side.

The helicopter took off. I could see Simon banging his fist on the side of the chopper door as he flew away. I gave him a jaunty little wave. Teach him.

Just then the cable that had been holding fast to Leikala's legs ripped out of the wall where it was attached and went whipping by me. Leikala was falling, and the statue was going with her.

CHAPTER TWENTY-FOUR

Still Hanging Around

Using my occasionally awesome catlike reflexes, I grabbed hold of the cable with both hands. I wasn't sure if I could hold her, but I had to try. I managed to wrap the cable around my arm and tried to stop myself from being pulled toward the edge of the roof.

"Alex!" I screamed. "Help me! Hurry!"

There was no question in my mind that I was going to go over the side. But I didn't. Instead I slammed hard into a pipe that was sticking up out of the roof. It hurt, but it stopped my momentum, and I was able to wrap the cable around the pipe to keep Leikala from falling.

I looked back at Alex. He and Dumber were struggling on the ground, and it looked like Alex was about to wear out.

Across the roof I saw Mr. Kim, Brent, and Pilar rushing out of the doorway. In a few seconds Mr. Kim had pulled Dumber off Alex and handcuffed him to one of the ventilation shafts. Mr. Kim had handcuffs? Sweet.

Brent and Pilar helped Alex get slowly to his feet. Mr. Kim helped me up.

"Are you okay?" he said. "I seem to keep asking you that question lately."

"I'm fine." I peered over the edge of the roof and saw Leikala hanging upside down. She was still holding the statue case, now with both hands. I couldn't resist.

"I didn't know you hung out here," I said.

Mr. Kim groaned, and Leikala shot me a dirty look. Mr. Kim grabbed the cable and started to pull her up, but she yelled at him to stop.

"Leave me alone! Let me go or I'll drop the statue!"

"Go ahead," I said. "Drop it. We couldn't care less about that statue. But I think your boss might be pretty upset with you if you did. You know what? Let's find out. Drop it. I would love to see it smashed to smithereens."

Down below I could see a bunch of police cars returning to the bank. Obviously they'd figured out that the whole gas-main thing was a hoax. Leikala could see them too. She had no way out of this.

"I'll drop it, I swear!" she said.

"Why do I have to explain everything to you twice? How did you ever get so high up in Simon's organization? I don't care if you drop it. I hope you do."

"Leave me alone!" she screamed. Apparently Leikala was a sore loser.

"You want to be left alone?" I said. "Fine. Mr. Kim, let's go."

Mr. Kim had a big coil of the cable in his hand. He let go, and Leikala dropped a couple of feet closer to the ground. She screamed.

"Stop! Don't drop me! Pull me up!" she yelled. Not so tough after all.

We pulled her up to the roof. Mr. Kim took the case away from her and then helped her to her feet. He took some of the cable and tied it around her hands behind her back. Apparently he was out of handcuffs.

We marched her over to where Brent and Pilar stood huddled around Alex, who was bent over catching his breath.

"Man," Alex said, breathing hard. "What do they feed those guys?"

He finally stood up straight.

"Brent, if you check the bottom of that statue, I think you'll find a small transmitter of some kind," I said. "That's how Simon figured out where it was."

Brent knelt down and pulled out the statue. Sure enough, there was a tiny little transmitter embedded in the base.

"Wow," he said. "Look how small this is."

He turned the statue toward us. We could just barely see the small black dot on the bottom of the base.

"Mr. Kim, I think you'll want to have this analyzed," Brent said. "This is the smallest transmitter I've ever seen. This is better than state of the art. I wonder how they got their hands on this? I mean, the power source applications alone! I'd love to see the microcircuitry on this! Can we take it back to Blackthorn with us?" Brent was starting to get all girly over this tiny little bug. It was kind of cute. He carefully put the statue back into the case and closed the lid.

"Why did you come after me again?" I said to Leikala.

She glared. "It was Simon's idea. If it were up to me, I'd have taken you to the deepest part of the ocean and dropped you in."

"It's good that we can discuss our feelings like this," I said. "Speaking of feelings, how does it feel to be hanging upside down off the roof of a four-story building while your great 'leader' flies away?"

She had no response to that. I win!

By then Detective Wanake and several policemen had made it to the roof. They led Dumb and Dumber and Leikala away in handcuffs. She yelled at me a few more times about how she would get me and I'd pay for what I'd done and blah, blah, blah.

"I'm sure they sell Oxy 10 in the prison commissary. That zit will be cleared up in no time!" I hollered after her. She tried to lunge away from the officers and come back at me, but they held her tight.

It felt great to see her dragged away by the cops.

Then Mr. Kim, that ruiner of special moments, spoke up.

"Rachel. I commend you on saving the statue. But what you have done here is wrong on so many levels. Sneaking out of the school. Stealing from your father's company—"

"I don't know what you're talking about," I said.

"Don't make it worse by lying, Rachel. Mr. Quinn was able

to trace your movements easily."

"Yeah, okay, maybe that's all true, but we *did* save the statue," I said. "Where would your precious little quest to take down Simon be if I hadn't done what I did?"

"My quest, as you call it, is not the most vital thing," he said. "Your safety and the safety of your classmates is of paramount importance to me. This is twice now you have gone off blindly into a dangerous situation."

Right there I got another big lecture about how impulsive I was, and how I needed to learn caution, and a bunch of other stuff that I tuned out because I bore easily. Yawn.

But that wasn't the worst part. After all we'd been through! After all the many positive things I'd done to thwart an evil would-be-world-taker-overer, Mr. Kim did the worst possible thing to me that he could.

He made us fly home the very next morning. No hula lessons for me.

CHAPTER TWENTY-FIVE

Can a Goddess, Like, Resign?

I was pretty steamed about the whole thing. I mean, okay. Mr. Kim was right. Technically, I did steal from my dad's company. And I suppose, just for the sake of argument, I could have tried to get the information to Mr. Kim and let him handle it without endangering my friends. But would it have killed him to let us stay in Hawaii a few extra days? I mean, we were already there!

However, there was one small point in my favor. Mr. Kim would never have been able to get the statue without me. No one but me could have walked through that wall of light. So when it was time for him to start handing out the punishments, I intended to remind him of that fact. Over and over, if necessary. No way would I let him lose sight of that.

Everyone on the plane knew that I was in a really grumpy

mood, so they let me sit off in a corner of the cabin by myself. I don't know how Mr. Kim arranged for the flight, but it was another charter jet. Probably belonging to the FBI or something. I sat there just staring out the windows, watching the clouds pass by. Every so often I'd hear Mr. Kim or one of the others murmur something, but we were all pretty tired, so the flight was mostly quiet.

I was about to doze off when Mr. Kim sat down in the seat across from me.

"Is this seat taken?" he said.

I looked at him with the best blank stare I could muster, then looked back out the window, giving him a grand view of my cold shoulder. I guess Mr. Kim had a right to be upset with me. But I sure didn't have to make it easy for him.

"Rachel, I understand that we are angry with each other. Don't you think it would be best to clear the air?" he said.

"Why? Your mind is made up. I'm sure you've got some punishment all worked out. Extra kitchen duty. Tae Kwon Do lessons at five-thirty instead of six A.M. Or are you just planning to put me out of your misery and send me home instead?"

"Rachel, I realize that you did what you thought was necessary. You were wrong, but you had your reasons. We need to discuss the decisions you make. And no, I'm not sending you home."

"Well, excuse me if that doesn't make me feel all warm and gooey inside," I said.

Couldn't he at least give me *some* credit for saving the statue? Throw me a bone, will you?

"By the way, Brent and Alex briefed me on what happened at Pele's Point. If it wasn't for you, that statue could not have been recovered. It was an incredibly brave thing you did."

Aha! Credit at last. But I knew Mr. Kim. There always had to be a however.

"However, don't you think you could have made a better effort to contact me? Or Mr. Quinn, or Agent Tyler?"

"How? How was I supposed to get in touch with you? We tried. Well, sort of. Okay, maybe we could have. But it didn't seem like there was time. If we'd waited till we heard from you, or until you came back, Simon could have found the statue. First you tell us we're involved in this. Then you go running off, telling us to stay out of it. Then we figure something out and—what? We're supposed to sit around and wait? I'm sorry, Mr. Kim. I'm just not built that way."

"But Rachel, your safety is—"

"Mr. Kim, with all due respect, I think we're way past the 'my safety' argument. I got captured by a psycho, fell off a giant piece of scaffolding, walked through a wall of mysterious light energy, and fought off a sword-wielding skeleton. Then, for good measure, I jumped out of a helicopter and almost got eaten by a shark. So the 'let's keep Rachel safe' discussion is a bit pointless."

Surprisingly Mr. Kim didn't have anything to say to that. Deep down, I think he knew I had a point.

"There's something else," I said.

Mr. Kim looked at me.

"Simon knows now that his copy of the *Book of Seraphim* is fake," I said.

The color drained from his face.

"Rachel, why would you—" he started, but I interrupted.

"I had no choice. He was going to kill Pilar. Apparently there's this prophecy in the fake book that says Mithras has to kill the one closest to Etherea. So he thought killing her would fulfill that, so I had to tell him the book was fake and that we changed all of it around. I had no choice. He had to know that part wasn't real. And by the way, whoever added that, thanks a lot! Like I don't have enough real prophecies to worry about."

Mr. Kim didn't say anything. He just looked down at his lap, a deeply troubled look on his face. A horrible thought flew into my head.

"That is true, isn't it, Mr. Kim? The part about 'Mithras taking that which is closest to Etherea'—you changed that part in the book, right? Tell me he's wrong."

I waited. Finally he spoke.

"What did Simon tell you? Be as specific as you can," he said.

"He went on and on about the *Book of Seraphim* spelling out the prophecy of the rise of Mithras, and that the first step is something like 'that which Etherea holds dearest must be taken from her,' which he figured meant he should sacrifice Pilar. So I told him to chill because he had the wrong book and he'd be getting stuff wrong if he killed her."

Again, the frown and the troubled look.

"Mr. Kim," I said. "What is it? I mean, he had it wrong. His copy of the book has been altered so he doesn't even have the correct prophecy, right?"

"I want you to remember I tell you this against my better

judgment," Mr. Kim said. "But I have decided you are right. If I ask you to trust me, I need to be completely honest with you.

"His copy *was* altered. However, most of the alterations were subtle changes in those sections that dealt with the location of the artifacts. We wanted to throw him off the trail. We put our emphasis on keeping him from finding those relics. And since it was a very difficult job to construct such a careful forgery, we had to be judicious. So the other parts of the text . . . have not been altered."

"Huh?" I said.

"According to the book, Flavius was instructed by Mithras to 'find that which is closest to the Goddess of Light and destroy it.' Scholars disagree on the details, but it's clear that Flavius believed Queen Naromi was the living incarnation of Etherea. The night before their last battle, he sent assassins into her fortress to murder her beloved sister, Princess Dharom. Etherea was enraged with grief, and it is said that this rage led her to defeat Flavius in battle."

"Okay. Fine. Great story. But I don't see what this had to do with me. All this happened thousands of years ago, and if you ask me, those people seem a little crazy. Besides, I'm not Etherea 'reborn.' I wasn't 'reborn' at all. I was just plain born. So I don't see why you're so worried."

Mr. Kim shook his head.

"That's why the book is so complicated and difficult to understand. In many ways the entire text is a massive riddle. You must understand the subtleties of the Kuzbekistani language. The English word *reborn* is a translation of the

Kuzbekistani 'charlom,' " Mr. Kim said.

"So?" I said.

"*Charlom* has more than one meaning in that language," he said. "It also means chosen." And he looked at me to make sure that I got it.

And so help me, I did. And I didn't like it. Because it meant that I didn't have to be reborn as Etherea; I could have been *chosen* to be her, later on. Just like Simon was Mithras' *chosen*. Somewhere, somehow, some dark forces had picked the two of us to act out this little drama. And if that was true, then the part about "that which was dearest" being taken from me was also true. And that meant— I looked at Mr. Kim.

"No," I said. Tears started flowing from my eyes, and I couldn't stop them.

For if this was all true, then someone, one of those "dearest" to me, was going to die. And if Queen Naromi wasn't able to stop it and she was, like, queen of a whole country, what would I be able to do? How could I save Pilar?

"But . . ." I tried to dry my eyes. "How can you tell if someone is chosen? I mean, how do you know Simon is Mithras and not just crazy?"

"Because I saw it happen," he said. Oh. "When Simon fell into the Mithrian temple and I went in after him. Simon and I spent about an hour exploring the temple. It was quite fascinating, really. It was remarkably well preserved for being abandoned in the desert for thousands of years. Simon was awestruck. He took pictures and seemed unable to pull himself away from the place. Still, we were on a mission and I reminded him that we needed to get back to our camp. He agreed, but before we climbed out, Simon went up to the stone altar at the front of the temple, took a sheet of paper and pencil, and knelt to trace one of the carvings.

"But when he touched the altar, something very strange happened. First, a howling wind came up inside the temple and began to blow through the room and swirl sand around us.

"Then the large carving of the bull's head on the wall above the altar began to change. The eyes of the bull began to glow with an eerie red light, and the light grew brighter and brighter until it filled the temple. A ghostly sound, a moaning, seemed to come right out of the walls. Then a voice spoke in a dead language that I'd never heard. I admit that I was frightened. All this time Simon's hands were on the altar as if he were frozen in place.

"Then the voice stopped. It grew quiet and the wind fell and the light faded. After it was gone completely, Simon slumped to the ground, unconscious. It took me several minutes to revive him. When he finally came to, his eyes were dark and troubled. I asked him if he had heard the voice."

" 'Yes, I heard it,' he said.

" 'I couldn't understand it. I've never heard a language like that before,' I told him.

" 'I understood it perfectly,' he said.

" 'What did it say?' I asked.

" 'It said, "You are chosen. You shall free me." ' "

Well, if that wasn't enough to give you goose bumps. Mr. Kim told me that he didn't believe Simon at first. He thought maybe they had released some kind of primitive booby trap in the temple. Or maybe it was some type of hallucination; perhaps something in the air inside the temple had affected them.

Simon, however, was convinced that he had found or unleashed some force. As he studied what they had found and learned the history of what had happened to Mithras and the Romans, he became convinced that he was Mithras reborn in human form. Maybe he was. Maybe that was what the voice in the temple was telling him.

"You know the rest," he said. "He became obsessed with Mithras, and that obsession has led us to this moment."

"Yeah, well, maybe he is, but nothing like that happened to me. No wind, no howling, no voice in a weird language choosing me. I'm just me! So, I've upset Simon's plans a couple of times and gotten in his face and given him lip. That doesn't make me Etherea," I said.

Mr. Kim looked at his lap again. His body language told me that he had something else to tell me that I wasn't going to want to hear.

"NO!" I said, trying to keep my voice low. "No. Do you hear me? It's not true. It can't be."

"I'm afraid it is true, Rachel. You are Etherea. Etherea is you."

CHAPTER TWENTY-SIX

If I Can't Resign, Then I Quit

"Well, I don't want to be," I said. "I unchoose me."

"Rachel." Mr. Kim spoke quietly and his voice was as gentle as a whisper. "It is your destiny. In life there are those who are given many paths from which to choose and those who are given only one. You must walk this path. It is who you are."

"You're wrong!" I didn't want to hear this anymore. Alex, Brent, and Pilar were kind of coughing and fidgeting in the front of the plane like they were desperately trying to hear what we had to say.

"Can they join us?" I asked Mr. Kim.

"Of course, but Rachel, you must never tell any of them, especially Pilar, what I've just told you about that part of the prophecy. It is for the best if we keep that from them," he said.

Great, so I get to bear all of this by myself. So far being a goddess pretty much sucked.

I waved them to take seats near us, and then I told them that Mr. Kim and especially Mr. Nutcase Blankenship were completely mistaken. That fruitcake could think that I was this Etherea person all he wanted. But I was definitely not her. No way, nohow.

They all looked at each other with expressions of discomfort on their faces.

"What?" I said. "What? Why is it I feel everybody knows something I don't?"

"Rachel, we saw it," Alex said.

"Saw what?" I said.

"What you did," said Brent.

"What are you talking about? What did I do?"

"You made the flashlight light up. And you were the only one who could walk through the wall of light," Alex said.

Well, shoot. In all the excitement I had forgotten about that part. It kind of put a hole in my "I'm definitely not Etherea" theory. Stupid facts. Still, there *could* be some other explanation. Sure.

"I got strange energy readings of you with the spectroscope," Brent said. "Somehow your body was giving off an electromagnetic charge that was the exact same frequency as that wall of light in the cave. That's why you could pass through it and none of us could."

"Well, that's a handy and marketable skill," I said. "Wait until the boys at college find out about that. I'm sure I'll have no trouble getting dates." I wanted to scream. "I thought you said it was static electricity from the lava or the iron in the volcano or the rocks in my head or something. How do you even know you were reading that thing right?" I said.

"I was," said Brent, trying not to look insulted.

"Rachel, Etherea was the Goddess of Light. She had—" Mr. Kim started to say.

"I KNOW SHE WAS THE FREAKING GODDESS OF LIGHT! Okay? You've told me that a million times! But I am not her!"

Truth was, I didn't care about the goddess part. I cared about the "my best friend getting killed" part. I couldn't be around her. I would have to leave, quit the Academy and go home, or back to Juvenile Detention, or hop a train to Costa Rica or something. Because that freak was out there, and if I stayed he was going to try to kill my friend. I would have to convince everyone that all of this was just one giant mistake. Maybe I would send a letter to Blankenship, telling him that I was resigning as the Goddess of Light. If he had any problems with that, he could take them up with the Gods and Goddesses Review Board, or Mt. Olympus, or wherever reincarnated gods went to resolve their disputes. And, to be safe, I would just disappear.

Then, of course, they delivered the death blow to my last desperate hope of denying my destiny.

Mr. Kim got up and went to the front of the plane. He opened his briefcase and took something out of it.

"There's something you need to see," he said as he walked

back toward me. "A few years ago we found this in Dharom, Kuzbekistan. Dharom is the city named for Queen Naromi's sister." He handed me a photograph.

I looked at the temple photo. It showed all kinds of carvings and stuff in the rock walls. In the middle was a base for what had been a statue, but now there were just feet and legs attached. The statue had either crumbled over time or been destroyed by looters or something. There were words carved into the pedestal.

"Do you see the symbols carved into the base of the statue?"

I could see Ραχηελ Λειγη Βυχηαναν carved there, but I had no idea what I was looking at.

"When those symbols, which are in the ancient Kuzbekistan alphabet, are translated into the modern Kuzbekistani language, the closest translation is the phrase *chaaba churl leghenin*. In English the closest translation is 'She conquers darkness.'"

"So? I don't get it," I said.

"Neither did I at first," said Pilar. "But then Alex and Brent told me about what happened in the cave and with the flashlight."

Pilar picked up a pad of paper she'd been holding on her lap.

"It's an anagram, Rachel. *Chaaba churl leghenin* is an anagram for Rachel Leigh Buchanan."

That was when I fainted.

CHAPTER TWENTY-SEVEN

I Am So Out of Here

We were back at the Academy and walking through the atrium. It was late at night and the place seemed almost deserted. I felt like I had been in shock ever since Mr. Kim showed me that photograph. How could my name end up on a statue from thousands of years ago? It had to be some kind of weird coincidence. *Coincidence* became my favorite word. I just chanted it in my head over and over again. Like a mantra. *Coincidence, coincidence, coincidence.* Somebody just carved some random letters years ago, that was all. Just one big two-thousand-year-old coincidence. Blankenship thought I was Etherea because he needed an enemy for his twisted little game to work. But I just couldn't believe this stuff about me. There had to be some other explanation.

Those carvings on the base of that statue could mean anything. Maybe it was translated wrong. For all anyone knew, that carving could be an ad for a local pizza joint.

Alex and Brent and Pilar went on ahead down toward the residential wing. I stopped to tell Mr. Kim my plan. I thought I would wait until Pilar went to class in the morning, then pack up and leave. I didn't have much stuff anyway. I would leave her a note telling her I had decided Blackthorn wasn't for me after all. Then I'd have Mr. Kim put me on a plane to somewhere. With all of his contacts, there had to be someplace I could hide. That way Pilar would be safe. That was all I cared about.

What a pitiful goddess I made. Goddesses should go out and kick some butt. Instead, I would be the goddess of running and hiding.

Just as I was about to share all this with Mr. Kim, we heard Pilar scream. A very loud scream. It filled me with terror.

Mr. Kim and I took off down the hall toward our room. Alex and Brent had heard it, too, and came running back from the boys' wing. We burst into my room and saw Pilar standing there, looking terrified.

"What is it, Pilar?" said Mr. Kim.

Pilar pointed to my desk. Since my desk tends to be kind of messy, at first I didn't notice what she was pointing at, but then I saw it. We all did. It was a smaller version of the gold medallion that Simon wore, with the carving of a bull's head. There it sat, big as life on my desk.

"He's here," Mr. Kim said. "Mithras was here!"

And there it was. Blankenship had proved that he could reach out and get me wherever I was. And it made me realize a few things—like how he always knew where we were going to be and what we were up to. Somehow, someway, he'd managed to infiltrate Blackthorn Academy. He had someone on the inside. And now he was so intent on destroying us, he didn't even care if we knew that. He wanted to mess with my head. Well, he was doing a really good job of it.

I also realized that I really didn't have a choice here. Like it or not, I had to finish this thing. If he could get to me here, he could get to me anywhere, and even me disappearing might not stop him from going after Pilar. So the only thing I could do was fight him. I needed to stay here, where Mr. Kim had my back, and where I could watch over Pilar. I was going to make that creep suffer. He was going to wish he'd never met me.

We all stood there, too stunned to know what to say. Suddenly I thought of something.

"The book!" I shouted. I turned and ran out the door and back toward the atrium and Mr. Kim's office. All of them followed behind me. It seemed like we were running in slow motion. Like time had slowed down somehow because we were afraid of what we might find. We shot into Mr. Kim's office. I ran to the bookshelf, flipping the little picture frame forward on its spring. The door popped open and we all went down the stairs, down and down and down, until we opened the door and burst into the situation room and saw that our worst fears had been realized.

The wall safe where Mr. Kim had kept the book was standing wide open.

The *Book of Seraphim* was gone.